T0361511

MY LESBIAN NOVEL
RENEE GLADMAN

DOROTHY, A PUBLISHING PROJECT

"The book rearranges itself in your life."
Danielle Vogel, *Between Grammars*

I

I: How will you start the novel you wish to write?

R: Currently, I'm dreaming up two novels, but this one—the one we're here to talk about—is the more challenging of the two. It will take place in a city, which isn't new for me as a writer. I've always loved cities. There will be lovers. Also not new. But I will try to do something different with how it moves. Usually when I write a novel, I know it's a novel because I'm writing with a feeling of ongoingness: I write outward, toward a shape, filling in a shape, though I wouldn't be able to say what that shape was as I was writing. In this new novel, the path has to be more defined. I want someone to meet someone else. Normally, I want people to meet, but as they're passing from one place to another. They don't stay together very long; we hardly know where they've come from, where they're going. Sometimes the two people have sex. One time two characters had sex for a long paragraph. This was in *Event Factory*. Usually, though, it's no more than a sentence. In this novel, I want to slow everything down. I'll start the novel by going to the beach with someone; I'll start on an airplane, in an attic apartment. I'll sit on a bench in a park for a week. I'll start because I need to leave a place, because I've been looking around for this story I can't find or can't get enough of or because it doesn't unfold the way I'd like it to.

I: Yes. But I'm wondering how you would begin to compose the space of the novel, particularly one that feels so foreign to you.

R: Why do you see it as foreign?

I: Well, it sounds like you want to write a story, and I wouldn't characterize your previous novels as stories with plots per se. What will you say to begin?

R: I will begin by trying to see who's there:

My memory is failing. I can't tell you shit about people I knew back when I knew them. I can recall all the names of the people sitting around this table, but that's because I've just met them. They are strangers to me. We are thirteen builders in a room, trying to solve a problem; we begin to address the problem by introducing ourselves. We say our names; we say which department we're from. And I grab each name and place it in a brightly lit space in my brain and whenever I get the chance I call out the name of one of these others in this room and I puff out a little bit when

I see I've impressed them. No one is as good as I am at this game. This is one of the things I do to feel myself in the world. Sometimes I lose track of all the markers that set my borders and I seem to just ooze out in the street, staining everything in my path, becoming faintly everywhere such that when I need to assert an opinion or remember something Ellis and I did when we were in London I don't have enough of me to make a form or see a form that might approximate a memory. I'm not saying I'm without memory. It's more that, as I near my forties, I notice I'm losing hold of some of the detail of my experiences, and it's the details that make the borders.

For example, I was walking down Broadway about a week ago on my way to J for a coffee. It was one of the mornings I worked from home. However, for me to actually work at home I have to leave the apartment every two hours. I need something: espresso, air. I need to look at a book. I need to meet my best friends, Esther and Marcel, for lunch. My job requires me to go look at a building from time to time, particularly when I'm working from home. In any case, this was my first time venturing out for that day. Autumn is my favorite season, especially late October when I've settled into my basic uniform: beautiful tweed blazer, deep-cut V-neck T-shirt, my skinnies, and blond leather boots. My hair is wild. I was waiting for my espresso when I heard a woman say "June?" in a British accent. Odd British. I didn't think fully British.

Hmm. I've put myself in an awkward situation. June is a straight-up girl, isn't she? I have no idea how I'll write her.

I: Do you know why you've chosen to tell the story from her perspective?

R: I think she builds models for an architect.

I: That makes you feel like you know her?

R: I'm not sure. It's too early to tell.

I: Okay. Fair enough. We'll return to this question later. What about some of these other people you named? Who's Ellis? Esther and Marcel?

R: Ellis is the boyfriend of June. It's so strange to write that word— "boyfriend." I have never written this word before in a fiction. I guess, too, most of the straight women I know have husbands now; everyone else in my world maybe says "partner." But, here, Ellis is definitely June's boyfriend.

I: Why is *this* something you know about June?

R: June is very smart. She grew up in the East Village, daughter of an artist and an engineer. She's been around a lot of different kinds of people. All her life. But her milieu is very heterosexual. She's progressive. But she isn't queer the way so many straight people are queer these days. Old-school straight with wild hair.

I: Is she African American?

R: I don't know yet. I can't figure it out. This is one of the reasons it's taken me so long to begin this novel. Ordinarily, I never get so close as to need to say what a person looks like. I'm always looking at them down a tunnel. Plus, my characters are usually Ravickian. No one asks me what they look like. I can't imagine what readers picture when they're reading about Ana Patova and her friends writing their books together. What do you picture?

I: You mean of their faces?

R: Yes.

I: They're a little blurry. It's more that I have ideas about what they look like. Ana Patova has a knot of hair. She's five-eleven, pretty collarbones, thin. Luswage has wavy brown hair. She's shorter, stocky, older. The one that disappears has a round face; he's a little chubby. One of the guys is really old; he has a long gray ponytail.

R: So, they're white?

I: Not necessarily. Interestingly colored. Darker. Not black, though. You do say they're Eastern European.

R: I do say that. It's a strange impulse. So perplexing that we can look down and see our bodies; we see our arms and legs but never our faces. We see other people's faces. If it weren't for the mirrors in my life, I might think I look like Danielle, since it's her face I see the most. But, I do want readers to recognize June. She's beautiful in an understated way. Not everyone sees it. But for those who do they find her breathtaking. Her lips are full. Her hair is wild. She loves a man. His name is Ellis.

I: Can you give me a sample of what a scene between them looks like?

R: In the language of the novel, or do you just want me to describe what they're like together?

I: Well, I'm curious how the novel would articulate them.

R: Okay. There's this:

Ellis and I walk through the city like many other couples some years removed from hipsterdom. Our bodies still slender and fashionable but perhaps moving about less boldly, less on than we'd been before. The paths we take are all lit and, because we're both successful, they often feel carpeted. I squeeze his ass as we walk the Highline and he squeezes my ass. "It's a little sleepy," I confess to Esther, who's currently single and says I should be grateful for the "peace" we've cultivated. Ellis and I are going to eat macro greens and steamed salmon in the Village. We're talking about his friend Charles's bid on a brownstone in Harlem. I'm looking out of my face at passersby. I think we must be beautiful to some people, enviable. We want to buy a place and I don't mean a closet. But even if you're doing well in this city you've got to be getting on astronomically to afford something that makes you feel like you're living large. We need a lot of windows. I do. I need to be high above the street. I want a room to sleep in and a bright room for building. I want brick and chrome. When I ask Ellis what he wants, he says, "Closets," then he says, "Season tickets," because Charles has season tickets for both the Yankees and Knicks. And Ellis and Charles are locked in some kind of battle that's at least fifteen years old. You can tell by the way everyone's walking that they're all expecting something good to happen tonight. I feel rather more caught up in something winding down, as if it were Sunday evening and work was resuming tomorrow. But it's Thursday night. I'm here. I touch his shoulder as we wait for the light to change, now back at street level. He looks down at me. His eyes are loving. I try to hold his gaze, but I can feel myself flickering. "Listen, everyone keeps saying 'Schenectady,'" he says, and we wonder if something bad has happened. But it's just a confluence. And we move on toward the restaurant. "I'm going to have the salmon," I give my order to the server who's always here on Thursday nights. "We're all trying to be healthy," he responds as he usually does in an unaffected voice. I think he's being sincere but is weighed down by depression or allergies. I haven't had the chance to ask him which. I can tell Ellis wants to have sex tonight. This is good. He's having miso. I'll take his penis in my mouth. It'll have a nice flavor. We eat so good.

I: Okay. Wow. Things are going to get raunchy?

R: There are certain things I want to put in language. But I often prefer to leave them incomplete, for them to crackle at the frayed end—something between me and the page. I have no idea what a penis in the mouth is like. However, a penis in June's mouth in a sentence; I experience that like a vein jumping under my skin. I'm new at this.

I: I just thought of this. It's a strange question. But how many scenes do you think one needs to make a novel?

R: You can't really ask that because there are so many different kinds of novels. How could one rule cover all the needs of narrative? I think, though, what you're asking is how few scenes can you have and still call what you've written a novel?

I: Yes. Something like that. Suddenly, I felt like your novel might only need one scene.

R: I think about this in relation to how one builds a story—what the materials for building are. I want to write a romance. How many scenes do you need of my characters at work or making dinner? I guess you build the world until it feels like it can hold up your purpose. Readers want to have confidence that the characters are moving through time. Maybe we're all just trying to figure out how everyone else gets through the eventless hours of the day. I find it hard to pretend like something is happening all the time. I resist, in fiction, the notion that you must write the boring stuff to make the parts you're excited to write about more believable. If something makes you go dim, I think you should avoid it. I never thought my lack of interest in plot made the novel form unavailable to me. I took it as an exciting challenge to find other sources of ground and propulsion. Now that I'm writing a more conventional story, I've got to reconsider plot. Can I find a way to get pumped up about it?

I: What's your problem with plot?

R: There's a way of writing where one's primary focus seems to be shaping the experience of the reader, laying out tracks that direct the emotional trajectory of how one comes to know the story. The part that bothers me in this kind of construction is where "discovery" belongs only to the reader. For the writer, there is a plan. Everything has been determined before the writing begins. So the writing itself is about manifesting the design masterfully. I see the value in that. I love architecture and maybe this is also how architects work. But I want to be a kind of reader as I write. That means not knowing what's up ahead. Yet I think when you're writing a romance you've got to line things up a little more. You've got to put two friends in a car and have them drive out of the city for the weekend:

Marcel and I have been driving for about an hour when I bring up the subject of my memory loss. I'm talking slowly because it's a little rainy outside. We're headed to Hudson to our friend Ramona Williams's first solo show. But the roads are slick and Marcel's only a so-so driver. "I'm an amazing driver," he says.

What's happening to my memory—I'm trying not to overreact—is unsettling. People I talk to say no one remembers everything, and I can see how that is true, but that's not really what I'm talking about. It's less about what I've forgotten than it is about what some of the memories I have look like, how they feel inside me. This morning, I was slicing shiitake mushrooms to make a tart for the picnic we were hoping to have on the way up, before the rain started, which was not predicted. I never wonder if I've misremembered something like that: I have an indelible engraving in my mind of the day's weather. Numbers and names burn brightly. But the mushrooms seem the closest representation of what memories look like; they're another kind of fungus. What I'm trying to tell Marcel is that most of my past acts like it's covered with fungus, growths that distort details, that change the shape of the emotions belonging to certain events. First, I thought the fungus was time, what time looked like in the body—it seemed reasonable that time would go on acting on something that was completed—but was time this invasive?

Wouldn't time want the event to remain recognizable? Marcel wants to say something he's not saying. Instead of looking out the window, which may suggest to him I'm done with the conversation, I look down at my hands. But I'm listening to the rain. It's soft. It sounds like a long novel: someone sitting on a hill, watching a dirty freight train passing through the landscape. "You really think memories look like mushrooms?" I love his voice. "I think returning to memory does; the reaching back is fungal." More of that novel about the train. Marcel and I have been friends for nearly fifteen years. I bought one of his first large-scale paintings, probably worth several hundred thousand today. He's the reason Ellis and I went to London in the first place.

I: Can you say what she's trying to remember without spoiling the plot?

R: I would love to answer that question, but if I do it changes what happens next in the book.

I: You're writing the novel as we talk?

R. We talk then I write.

I: What does your writing space look like?

R: It's my memory palace. I work in a large bright room that I've filled with flat files, many of which are at least a decade old. They're expensive (though some I purchased second-hand), and it's taken me years to fill the room. On top of the files are wooden boxes where I place tiny drawings and photographs, which act like keys in my vocabulary. A drawing releases a word in my mind, and that word points to some fact or question I want to preserve.

I: So you and June share this problem with memory?

R: Something is happening to June that's beyond memory loss, and if that were happening to me, I'm not sure I'd be writing a novel about it. I definitely wouldn't be building a memory palace, because that's not what they're for.

I: Why *are* you building one?

R: Hmm. Let me back up. It's less that I'm building a memory palace than that I'm conjuring a certain kind of architecture in which to write. Something like an index, but physical. Three-dimensional. An index to sit within.

I: So whose memories are being indexed?

R: Correction. I sit in a hive of writing. Yeah, it's not a palace or an index. Forget everything I said about flat files. It's a bright, empty room, full of voices.

I: Okay. Do you want to say anything about the voices?

R: Let me make some words:

Sometimes I find myself in a space full of so many brown faces I feel like I'm in another country. Even in New York, once you enter a place, things tend to go white. All different kinds of people walk the streets, but only white people enter certain buildings. Even in Brooklyn, where I find myself more and more often. But, in Hudson, I never would have expected to see all these beautiful people. Where are they from? I've left Marcel to talk to some Chelsea gallerist (there's only so much of that I can take: they're talking about a male artist who smashes up trucks and cars into little boxes). I've done one circuit to take in Ramona's paintings, which are nearly impossible to engage in such a crowded room, so I begin a second tour. It's not just that there are so many black people here; it's also that they are beautiful in a revelatory way. I want to catalog what everyone is wearing. I'd like to build an architecture for this way of being. A building for these clothes. This bright relaxedness. I try to stand outside myself to see what I look like among them. Do I look bright? Alternative? Soft and distinctly other? It's an otherness without anxiety though, as if buried deep in their pockets they each have a tiny card that says they belong.

Ramona paints these circles that look rusted. They are rings of fire, whose color leans toward embers rather than full flame. Something dark, finishing, and ancient, but still vivid at its center. This current exhibition is a series of eleven spectacularly large rings, each painted on vertically oriented canvases at 84 x 77 inches. They are paintings, but they look like drawings to me, still in motion, still thinking. They are exquisitely inexact spheres. I want to get closer so I can see what she's done to make each its own, but at an opening this is virtually impossible. The energy of the crowd is high and magnetic, forming boulder-shaped clusters of loudly chatting art enthusiasts that inadvertently guard against viewing the work we're all there to celebrate.

I think I have engineered a way to get my face directly in front of one of the paintings. It requires that I stand within a circle of people, a few of whom I've spoken to before, and smile and say "Congratulations" to a tall man, who is very happy with himself. I do this. It's not hard, people are feeling generous tonight. After a few moments, my calculations come to bear. The woman standing next to the happy man rises on her toes to kiss his cheek, creating a small opening for me. I slip through and acquaint myself with Ramona's Circle #6. *The marks that form the circle are more complicated up close. It's more than the hand making a curving line; there are many multi-directional curving lines moving with the general outlook of a circle. And it feels like if I had a magnifying glass those many curving lines would be revealed to be doing something else.*

Marcel interrupts my study to introduce me to someone I already know. His name is Glen and he's a framer. We tell Marcel we're acquaintances

*and laugh, bring glasses to our mouths. There's a fourth, too. A woman
no one is introducing to me, who I also think I know.*

*"Do you remember me?" She steps closer; we make a parenthesis. Glen
and Marcel carry on about kombucha, where you can find it on tap in
the city. I feel very tired, like I'm pressing the world down inside me.
We are surrounded by burning circles, even if all the disturbance in the
room leaves the circles burning without anyone seeing them, not for any
significant amount of time anyway. A buzz of conversation, plus what I
think is Sonny Rollins's* Saxophone Colossus, *playing on repeat. She has
a faint British accent.*

I: You're done?

R: For now.

I: It's interesting that twice now you've cut off the narrative when the
British woman approaches June. What's going on there? And can you
talk about June's relationship with Marcel? I noticed some tension
there. What does she mean she "loves his voice"?

R: But, you see, you must remember where we are. We're inside June.
She doesn't know she's a novel; she's just in her body feeling what she
feels. His voice is deep and syrupy, like he's listened to jazz and blues
his whole life, like maybe he plays the clarinet, pulls a hum out of

wood. So, she's in her body next to this sound and it's coming from her friend who's letting her say, "My memories are becoming like mushrooms," and the worst he might do in this moment is chuckle because both words start with *m* and he's always noticing these things, and right here she recognizes that: I love his voice. It's innocent, mostly. Did I say that Marcel is married? He has a two-year-old. His wife is an actress; someone you know.

I: What does Marcel look like?

R: Hmm. Black hair, black stubble. Very handsome. Kind eyes. Not incredibly tall. His mother is Spanish, his father Mexican. He grew up in Chicago, but he's been in New York at least twenty years. Forty-five. Wears a denim jacket until the temperature falls below thirty. Loves thick wool scarves, which he collects in Europe. His favorite is a deep teal color. I see him quite clearly. He's a pretty boy, but Catholic, so he just wants to make a home. Painter. Builds furniture.

I: But June you can't see as plainly?

R: When I think of June it's like I'm looking out of my face. Soon, perhaps, I'll bring her to a mirror. We'll have to see. In the meantime, her lips are full; her hair is wild. She dresses a bit androgynously, though the jackets always have a feminine cut, and her boots are narrow-toed. Still, she prefers blazers and jeans to dresses. Esther is like this too. We haven't gotten to her yet. She's coming.

—

I: So who's the British woman?

R: Well, I want to answer your original question as to why the chapters break off when she appears.

I: Okay . . .

R: I was just thinking . . . I haven't entirely given up the idea of writing blindly. Something happened in London and this woman seems to be at the center of it, but I don't know the details. I'll have to write to find them:

At breakfast this morning at T on 10th Avenue in Chelsea, I open to the first page of the journal I kept that summer we were in London. For the past few nights, I've woken out of a dense dream where I'm inside an enormous ball of thread, as if cocooned, and the ball is in motion, moving alongside cars down some central road (I can't see the name through the slits in the ball), and the ball's going as fast as the cars, maybe racing them. But my problem is I'm not driving the ball; no one is. I'm alone. The light inside is red. I guess the thread is red, and sunlight enters through the slits, like windows, but very very small windows that make it hard to see. The windows are just about making me feel that the ball is also a kind of light bulb. The ball spins down the busy street, makes turns; it even stops at lights, although this appears infrequent. And, except for when we're stopped (we seem to always break with me in an upright position), I spin as the ball spins, and this makes me feel (in the dream) as though someone is singing inside my head: dizziness as a weird serenade. I wake with my legs clenched, my abdomen tight, my hips slowly bucking. I'm coming. And I have the sensation that I've just said a name out loud that isn't Ellis, but my mouth is too far away from my brain to know whose name I did call. Everything is still. I reach for Ellis, but he's already left for work. No, I remember, he's at a meeting in Chicago.

Later, when I'm up and dressed, the memory of the dream returns to me. We were in London sixteen months ago; I have no idea why I've been thinking so much about that time. In fact, I'm not even sure what I'm thinking when the memories come to me. They come in fragments, stretched and hazy. So, after eating, I start re-reading my journal, look-ing for clues, something to put all these pieces in order. I'm also looking for traces of whose name I may have called.

My entries are short. "I spent all day at the Tate Modern viewing the Ag-nes Martin show; met Ellis for wine at Bouquet (crowded; we sat on the curb; three small streets ending at our table). More later. So much to say." The first three entries end with these same words: "More later. So much to say." But when I sit to think about our week there, as I am now doing, I find that it just wasn't that spectacular of a trip. I walked for hours, crossed many neighborhoods, barely covering a quadrant of the city. Ellis attended a conference for much of our time there. We always met at Bou-

quet in the evening to spend some hours together before sleeping. I was drinking a dry, sparkling rosé most nights. The fish was amazing.

Another entry reads: "I eat a different fish every night. Last night we were in Fitzrovia. I was surprised to see so many tourists there. We talked to a couple from Australia who wanted to go out dancing. Did we want to join them? There was something a little too shapeless about them. We walked back to our place." Going with them might have made the trip more remarkable. I keep reading.

There's a long entry toward the end of the week that is all atmosphere, as if I'm writing a novel about something I can't name directly. It embarrasses me. The passage is dense with nature descriptions, taking note of changes. I write that I'm standing on the bank of the Thames counting birds flying above the water versus birds on the water versus birds diving into the water. It reads like I'm trying to work myself into a trance, "Everything is spinning in London, the clouds are moving faster than they should; something rises as something slopes, bridge enshrouded." And then the writing trails off, ends in a fragment: "hazy fallen bodies."

I hate when I keep secrets from myself.

I: What did you learn?

R: I remember when I was younger, I didn't have many words for the things I felt. I'd write all this language around the thing but never say the thing or the thing at first remove from the thing, because that would be too close. People would find out. But because I didn't really know what I needed to say, I didn't exactly grasp what I was cloaking. So, I was never sure if I was quite cloaked.

It was time to call Esther, who doesn't teach on Monday or Wednesday. We arranged to meet at a bookstore on Spring Street, where she's spent most of the morning searching for a "certain kind of book" she hasn't yet found so is open to the interruption. I tell Esther the same thing I told Marcel about the mushrooms. We've walked into a new shiny café to have espresso. And I'm waiting for her response. People for some reason aren't terribly shocked when you tell them your memories are like mushrooms. I think we are all so used to poetry. That is, to encounters with alterity. We use our brains all the time, so metaphors catch on. Esther teaches art history and practice: she is always talking about lightning rods and pigments. So, I say, "Trying to remember things has become fungal for me," and she raises her second espresso to her mouth, holds her hair back from her face. I know she wants to suggest herbal remedies, but I think she can see that I'm more troubled than usual. I feel like I'm confessing something, but it's more like confessing placeholders for secrets because I really don't feel that I have any. I have stuff I do in private, but nothing treacherous or super perverted. "Esther," I think this is the right thing to ask, "what was I like when I came back from London? Was I weird in any way?"

—

"You mean when you and Ellis went years ago?"

"It was about sixteen months ago."

"But so much has happened since then." She's talking about her life, though. Her second book came out half a year ago. "All I remember are line edits."

We decide to split a quiche with caramelized onions and sweet potatoes.

"That was when we kept doing the walking tour in Central Park, right?"

"I think so," I tell her. "When I try to put myself back there, everything is strangely hazy. Like a building has collapsed on itself and I've got to lift all these shards and slabs of things in order to rescue what's underneath."

Esther says she remembers me walking down the line of the river, the Thames, she clarifies, and that's because I was laying it out in detail, immersed in its ecology. I kept saying the water was brown. The more we talk and eat, the more defined are her memories of what I told her about London. Eventually, she stops reminiscing and just studies me.

"Sometimes you seem like you're haunted," she reports, "as though you're reaching through something in order to talk to me."

"When was I last like this?" I ask her.

She looks up at the ceiling, as is her tendency when she needs space to think. "About three months ago, then maybe a year before that."

———

I prefer to look down at my plate.

"I think I met someone," I say slowly, fully exhausted.

"Hmm. You met that woman . . . she was a line artist. You were excited about her work. But you didn't mention any guys."

"She must be in New York right now."

"The artist . . . ?"

"Yeah. I don't remember her name. But I think I saw her the other night in Hudson. We were standing in a group of people, and she'd just turned to talk to me when someone interrupted us."

"Okay . . . what's the mystery here?"

"No mystery. Marcel just said something about me being checked out. I felt like I was seeing something flicker at the edge of myself but couldn't make it out. I hate art openings. There are always people there you're supposed to know who you can't remember, and they want to hold you close or, worse, air kiss you."

This is familiar territory that allows us to return to my fungal memory and her recent forays within the thrall of academia. We finish lunch with a glass of wine and don't return to that conversation. She wants to know about the Koebler house the firm is building outside Detroit. It has a suspended roof.

I: So, you go far away, and you meet someone who makes you lose your memory. That sounds kind of noir.

R: If by "you" you mean "one," then yes we're definitely in a story. This isn't about me. It's a novel.

I: Well, I was just thinking about how you said you've been struggling with your memory—

R: I'm pretty sure I said it was June who's struggling with her memory. I'm just struggling to write a novel. Although, it's true: I am interested in what time does to things that happened long ago when you try to reach back for them. How the details get rearranged, stained by surrounding memories.

I: You used the phrase "memory palace" earlier—

R: I know. But I want that concept to be more about architectures for thought than placing things so that you can recall them more easily. It would be great to be able to say "memory palace" and be talking about a novel space or a paragraph.

I: Okay, noted. I don't want us to get derailed. June seems to be having a pretty intense moment.

R: She's a mess.

I: Does the passage continue?

R: Yeah, just a little more to that chapter:

I've slept more than usual this week while Ellis has been in Chicago. At work, I've been tasked with solving the problem of an overhanging porch that seems too close to the stream that flows beneath it on the west side of the Detroit House. I keep drawing plans that look like they belong to some other reality, one with less gravity, and everyone's looking at me sideways. I'm just not paying the right kind of attention. My dreams leave me "gifts" from a raucous sleep: I find actual pieces of things in the bed but also find myself in the middle of narratives that I don't recall opening. I row a canoe down a river as it rains. I open a box under water. I'm designing a house to fit inside a refrigerator.

I start a new journal so that I'll have a record of whatever this is I'm undergoing. But I'm still combing the London journal. In fact, I found something curious this morning, almost as if a shadow passed through the retelling of an afternoon I spent at White Cube—

You know, I haven't written in months . . . not on this novel anyway. I wrote those last sentences about June's new journal yesterday, relieved that I'd found a way back in. Sometimes when I stop writing I'm sure I'll never write again, especially now that I'm drawing. And as I've been saying, writing this novel is not easy for me. Laying out crumbs like this, walking with my eyes open.

I: What have you been doing in the interim?

R: I've been working on a series of drawings that are the widest I've done yet (though I call them "long"); they are horizontally oriented, like most of my visual work, just about ten inches longer than I'm used to. I decided when these sheets arrived that I wanted to draw language charts on them. I made blue lines in pencil—an irregular chart, not uniform like a grid, more a chart with gaps, incomplete in whatever it's measuring—and, in the first drawings, I used pencil to write inside the lines, a light graphite. Then I made clouds out of this gouache that appears in many of the drawings: it's neutral gray mixed with water, maybe too much water, such that it becomes a light tan. Then I took this same paper and painted city-house shapes in black gouache; there are four in this series. I spread them out in the studio and just kind of looked at them a long time, asked myself if all the silence in me meant I should be writing instead of drawing. It's hard to convince myself that I'm only drawing when I draw, since at the core of it is writing. The hum I knew for years before I even drew my first line.

I: Did you think about the novel?

R: Yes . . . in a way I drew so that I could think about the novel, which I find more and more difficult to write. Drawing opens up space around me, both interior and exterior space; it kind of lifts me off the ground, turns everything into energy fields I call math.

—

I: Would you say this is a dream state?

R: No, June is in a dream state. I live in something emptier (when I am alone, when I'm working). It's crisp and bright but also remote and, as I said, empty. When I think of dreaming, I see it more as an occupation. Being full of atmospheres that have a different sense of time. June wakes, her body is ready for the day, but the dreams, or the "being in a dream," being dreamed isn't finished. I'm drawing so as to write but to stay silent.

I: Do I pretend like what you've just said makes sense and ask you about June or do I try to find out more about this idea of "drawing so as to write"?

R: Well, I've written about this a lot in the past few years. But I can briefly talk about the ways in which this practice has evolved. When I began drawing, I felt a direct correlation between the lines I was making and possible lines of prose I could be writing. Hence, my calling them "paragraph drawings" and, more publicly, "prose architectures." However, most of them didn't look like paragraphs: they had too much space inside them. But, for me, they held the time of writing, such that when I drew I felt that I was *inside* narrative, seeing narrative, seeing its very construction from within (as I describe exhaustively in *Calamities*). I would repeat in many different forums: this is language with its skin peeled back. But it wasn't just a project that finished with the publication of *Prose Architectures*; it was as if those marks I used to build that particular set of drawings became a new lexicon for me. I had always drawn buildings when I drew, but not until the first prose architecture drawing did I draw buildings in concordance with writing. Once I understood my lines and my scripts and my cities as forms of prose, I moved forward through them into subsequent drawings (on larger paper, incorporating gouache, watercolor, now acrylics), still preserving, developing this feeling, this awareness and engagement that I was still writing. Now when I'm drawing, it's less that I'm drawing the time of writing or investigating narrative per se as much as I'm going into the math of the space that frames and backgrounds writing. These are thinking spaces that take the form of charts, maps, energy readings. It's a very interior measurement. It's like being in the most inside of a thing or a question. Although I have never understood math, this is what I've thought math to be: a way of measuring the most inside of something.

I: But how does this process allow you to think about this novel specifically?

R: While I said to draw was to write, I should also say sitting in a kind of electrified stillness—how I see the posture of thought—is also writing. I often talk to Danielle about the big anxiety of my day as an artist: the need to make bridges from one part of the day to another, from one form of creating to the other, from sun to twilight, and within these major turns all the minute shifts that happen. Sitting in thought . . . I'm leaning into this buzz and that's where the novel exists. I'm asking all day: How do I put myself in the proper state to write out these dreams that have struck June, these weathers that move through her? When I'm drawing, I'm no longer still, but I am still leaning into the buzz. I'm trying to become porous.

I: And did it work? Are you now ready to go on with the novel?

R: Yeah, I think I have enough to move further now . . .

It is as if I have to fight my sleep to have my mouth with me. I have to fight my dreams, my subconscious, my blood—everything I can't see. My body responds immediately: alarm goes off, hand reaches for the phone, stops the sound, eyes adjust to the light of day, body senses, remembers, the lack of presence on the other side of the bed (Ellis traveling, where is he this time?), but the spirit lags. I don't know if this is the right word. I say "mouth" because spirit seems to enter and leave through the mouth. When I open, it is because I physically change the air in my body, and I do this by opening my mouth. And when I say I open, I mean I move my interiority toward the edge of me so that I can be in the day. I need my mouth: I see you by talking. I eat, I kiss, I fuck with my mouth. I make my models by talking. Is it morning? Something dark happened to the sky. Maybe a rain coming.

Griffin—a colleague also working on the Detroit House—texts me an address. I've got to get my body there. In preparation for our presenta-

tion to Shelia, the head architect, I need to study axiom handles for suspended asymmetric structures. It's my third study in as many days. The problem with my model is that we can't compensate height logistics when the water running beneath the master bedroom window is alluvial. Full of everything. There's a loft in Gramercy where the owners apparently had a creek built to flow through the home, and the water is piped in from some hidden aquifer to which maybe only very rich people have access. In the elevator down to the lobby, and as I begin to cross the city, I can't help feeling there's a wind circling me, trying to get me to go west instead: first my neck, then my waist, my wrists, my hips, knees. My boots are beautiful. They keep me on my path, but I feel naked. My mouth is in my belly, looking up the tunnel of my throat. Drop some coffee in me. But I don't know these cafés I pass.

There are all these secret wells beneath the city; at least that's what every exceptionally rich New Yorker tries to tell me. I meet one every couple of weeks in my work; not only because the wealthy are always trying to add impossible fixtures to their already impossible architectures, but also because the rich people you've already built for are always sending other rich people your way. Art collectors want to make inner sanctuaries behind their library walls; actors want their beds to float three feet above the floor . . .

The owner lets me in because I'm giving him something too. He's letting me measure his east-west ax handles and I'm doing a schematic to add a Thursor lip to his bathtub. The height to the ceiling is spectacular;

there's more ceiling than there is room. However, it's the interior wall that draws the eye. A woman crouches on the floor with her back to the room, a pencil in her hand.

I clear my throat, hoping not to startle her, although one of my favorite happenings in the world is stray pencil markings on walls. It's a soft clearing that I must perform twice before the woman notices I'm there.

"Oh hey," she says somewhat distantly.

"Hi. Sorry to interrupt." What can I say that doesn't sound stupid? "Do you need a ruler?" Ugh.

"No, I'm good. I'm just signing my name."

I look up at the blank wall above her and wonder where the drawing begins.

Griffin texts again: "How's it going? We need the numbers by 3."

And I have to pull myself away from the woman crouching with her pencil to remember what it is that I do, which is what she's doing but with the added ruler and less the signing of my name than making other smaller markings in a notebook. In a different room, too. I'm supposed to be in the bathroom, looking at the bathtub.

I: So, I think we should begin today by informing the reader that there's been a considerable break in time since we last met.

R: Oh, that's interesting. Why should we do that?

I: Well, I was thinking how when we read novels there's no real record of the time in which the novel was written. The pages run so smoothly, are so ordered, we probably don't put much thought to it. But since I'm talking to you as you build this novel, it seems like we're providing an opportunity for the reader to actually know how long a novel takes to be written and whether it's written with or without interruption.

R: Some novels are written fast. I've heard people talk about writing as a fever dream. Once I was at a reading and this writer was saying he checks into a hotel and writes and drinks and, I imagine, eats shitty food until he's done. Yuck, by the way.

I: Which part is "yuck"?

R: The part where writing is treated like an illness. For the record, I wish to *yuck* without judgment. People have all kinds of reasons for writing. I use writing to feel good, even if the subject of my writing is melancholy or dislocation. I love sublimation that feels like a very hot bath or the long runs I used to do. Sometimes I do a stretch that is almost a split and it releases so many endorphins I start giggling. I have always wanted writing to feel that way. But I know that's not what everyone or even most people want.

I: Does that mean you don't feel good when you're not writing?

R: I feel good if my body and brain are engaged at the same time. I like to hike even though Danielle makes fun of me because I don't see anything while we're hiking. She's stopping every few feet to take countless videos of woodland ephemera or water rushing down the same creek or just me leaning on my stick waiting for her to be done taking a picture of me leaning on my stick. It's not like I'm in my head, not seeing. I told her the other day, "I durate," which is obviously not a real word, but I mean "I experience duration while hiking." That's the thing I'm doing the most. Although, I am very aware of the fragile trees in our forest; a new one falls every day, it seems, and now hangs in the crook of another tree that is soon to fall. It's such a tender forest it feels like prose. I'm often thinking that, so I always miss the first sighting of the trout lily or the bounty of usnea, but it's hard to miss the skunk cabbages when they return to the forest. Oh, I was just trying to say that sometimes I forget I need to write to feel my best, and walking is a form of writing, as is drawing.

I: Do you mind if I say how long it's been since we met?

R: Sure. Fuck it.

I: When I first suggested we should tell the reader how much time had passed, it had only been a couple of months. But after you asked why I wanted to do that and I said it offers readers a glance into the time of writing, five years have passed. It's phenomenal.

R: We are still here. So much has happened.

I: I don't want to review the recent history of the world with you, in this space, but I am suddenly overwhelmed with questions about what you've been doing and thinking over this time. Can I say, too, something as understated as I'm glad you're still here?

R: Of course, and same. Not everyone is.

I: *Not everyone* ever is.

R: True. So how do I even begin to account for the past five years? As pertains to this novel, something kind of extraordinary happened. I think the first time we met to discuss my lesbian novel it was spring of 2018, and I'd just finished reading Naomi Alderman's *Disobedience* and Fiona Shaw's *Tell it to the Bees*. I can't remember how I'd gotten there, but I'd been taking a foray through lesbian fiction—I'd also read Doris Grumbach's *Chamber Music* and probably a Sarah Waters book. And was looking at their endings and feeling like, "Didn't we fix this? Didn't we advocate for happy endings for lesbians?" This was one place where I was unhappy with ambiguity. I think people who write literature (me included) are not comfortable with leaving people in a well-nourished and happy place. It's not complex enough. It seems to suggest all your questions have been answered. But we were a year and a couple months into Trump's presidency, and I wanted somewhere to go where I felt safe, and it was certainly not going to be a Beckett novel or any contemporary novel full of horrible things happening to somewhat horrible people told in an unaffected voice. But these lesbian novels were just as bad. The women in *Tell it to the Bees* get run out of town. Rachel Weiss's character in the book version of *Disobedience* is a player; she just walks away from the other Rachel. *Chamber Music* is a beautifully written book dominated by a wife and, toward the end of the story, a nurse taking care of a brilliant though ill man, who's a famous composer. After his death, the wife and nurse become lovers, but they only have a few years together before one of them dies! So, I was like, I'm going to write my own fucking lesbian romance, and when you finished reading it these women were going to be together and happy and sexy! The funny part is, I had no idea there was a lesbian romance genre full of Happily Ever Afters, HEAs, like hundreds of books, so many that I didn't even need to go back to Rita Mae Brown or to the nineties, when many of these books emerged, because they were being written now and profusely so. However, I didn't discover this until the fall of 2018, and for some reason, once I did, I could no longer write this novel.

I: Did you feel like you no longer needed to, because now you had all these options? Like, you could get that hit of HEA you needed without having to write it.

R: Perhaps, initially. I certainly did dive in. But I think it had more to do with the artifice of the interview. I hadn't necessarily wanted to write an *experimental* lesbian novel, and the more we talked, the less this felt like a conventional thing we were doing. I don't know if I expected the artifice to fall away, where I would just be writing June's story, but it never did, and talking to you became integral to how I imagined the story unfolding. The only way it could unfold.

I: Then what happened?

R: I don't know. I accepted an artist residency in Berlin for 2019. Went there and didn't sleep for a year. It was so noisy. I just stayed up all night reading, then stumbled around during the day, sitting on benches in old cemeteries, sometimes meeting up with people but largely walking the city on my own trying to figure out who I was in Europe. I started writing my second lesbian romance in the fall of 2019. By then, I'd become a scholar.

I: What does it mean to be a scholar?

R: It means I knew all the tropes. I'd read hundreds of books. Could name the popular authors. I could talk in detail about "ordinary" human emotion. I learned a lot about what femme lesbians wear, according to these authors. The kinds of heels a high-fashion lesbian would wear. I learned how much people who are not writing experimental novels have their characters eat pizza and watch TV. It was like getting a tour through a kind of living that had eluded me before. I was always weird—even as a kid—living a weird life. And although I would argue I have a great capacity for emotional response (in certain conditions), somehow reading these books taught me about the little things. Like all the ways a person can get their feelings hurt inadvertently, how the hurt blooms, and, if not consoled, which most of the time it isn't because the other person doesn't realize what they've done, what they've said or not said, how that leads to a great misunderstanding. I detest this . . . device? In romances. Hate it. But it did build in me a greater awareness of how destructive silence or avoidance could be. And, in better novels, I learned how people like to be consoled. It's weird, because I should have known these things, but I think maybe I was cynical toward them. I learned things about myself that I'm not sure I would ever have known had I not gone down this rabbit hole.

I: Can I ask what you learned?

R: Well, there's this one novelist, who doesn't do breakups and misunderstandings, which I deeply appreciate, but her MCs have a lot of past trauma—usually injuries, emotional or physical—and they get paired up with someone who, at one or two points in the story, lifts them off the ground or pulls them into their lap. Carries them when they are hurting. I am a sucker for women carrying each other around. So much of our pain is that old, where we could have been lifted and cradled by a caretaker and weren't. I love it. It pulls all my strings.

I: What else do you love?

R: In the genre?

I: Yes . . . as a scholar/enthusiast.

R: The shifter romance is probably my favorite. I love wolves and dragons. Wolves more because they are very protective, and they growl even in their human form when they sense arousal from their mate or when someone is threatening their mate. I also love a fake marriage trope. I love romances that take place on farms where there are many animals, especially horses and goats. I love a romance with a dog. Even more a dog and a toddler. It is so unlike me to admit these things, but I can't stop myself. I could go on all day about the books I've read and what of them I've loved and what I've hated, but I'm not sure it's as interesting to others as it is to me.

I: Okay. Maybe we can circle back later to some of the things you mentioned, but right now I'm curious about the second romance you were writing. How was it different from this one and did you finish it?

R: The second romance, unlike this one, has a title. It's called *Every Winged Creature*. Despite how it sounds, this is not a shifter romance. It's more about redemption and healing. Two characters—Mia and Dakota—cross paths when they are teenagers, when Dakota appears suddenly to defend Mia from a bully who's lost control of herself and is about to do deep bodily harm to Mia. Dakota intervenes and stomps the girl a bit. But because of her own trauma, she misinterprets Mia's look of gratitude and curiosity. She thinks it's a look of horror—Mia being horrified by her—and runs off in shame. Fifteen years later, Mia runs a bookstore across from a park and over a few days starts to take notice of a person sitting on a bench, looking worse for wear. Is that the correct saying? After exchanging a greeting on one of these days, Mia becomes preoccupied with where the woman goes at night. There's no way she keeps sitting on that bench. It's an alright neighborhood in terms of safety, but it's not utopia. One evening, on her way home from a shelter where she volunteers, she decides to check. And there the woman is, still sitting there. This is unconscionable for Mia. She approaches the woman and encourages her to come home with her. The woman—who if you haven't guessed is Dakota—is at the end of her rope (is that correct?—when you write romances you have to get very good at these sayings); she's come to the end of trying. Wants to go no further, wishes to die right there on the bench. Never anticipates someone like Mia—who glows and is kind and beautiful— extending a gesture of care toward her. In her mind, she's a monster. Too violent, unlovable. So, you can see where this story is headed. I love a protector/rescue storyline. I'm not sure if this is considered a trope. In any case, I wrote the first seventy pages of that novel very fast. I wrote up to the moment of their first kiss. It's the evening after they discover their prior connection, which is very dramatic and lovely and worthy of a few tears, and they're sitting on Mia's sofa and

Mia is staring at Dakota's lips (that happens a lot in romances); Dakota has had no experience with tenderness, so she's feeling pretty vulnerable, very much out of her depth, and doesn't understand why Mia would gaze at her like she's worth something (more tears may fall here), but she decides to trust Mia, or at least let go in this moment. They kiss, then I stalled.

I: I'm sensing a theme here. What makes it impossible to go on?

R: Honestly, I think it's the same problem I had with *Houses of Ravicka*, the fourth book in my Ravicka series. I reached a point where I exhausted discovery and non-knowing and found myself in a space of having to know. I couldn't stay at the same level as my narrator, not knowing where the missing house was; rather, it seemed I was being required to remove myself from the experience plane, decide what happened to this house and all the other mysteriously behaving houses of Ravicka, then return to the novel and set it up for the characters to discover while I am all the time knowing. Ugh.

I: Not a fan of the plan?

R: Not this kind of plan. For me, writing is improvisation. It's responding to problems of space created by the previous sentence in a paragraph or by the question of beginning (a new chapter, a new day or moment of perception). Knowing beforehand then laying it out, that's something else. I guess that's building, but that kind of building doesn't lead to the kind of architectures I want to occupy or sign my name to. I want mine to be alive, responsive, and impossible.

I: What is your wish for *Every Winged Creature*? Are you prepared to leave it unfinished?

R: I really don't like to do that. Those books haunt me. I end up having to write other books about how I couldn't write those original ones. I keep trying to find someone who will finish it for me, someone who loves to write drama and resolutions. We'll see.

I: Definitely. Well, we took a bit of a detour after revealing the five-year gap in our conversation and in the progression of June's story. Hearing what you did over the time we were away and learning how your relationship to romances has evolved does bridge the gap somewhat. Although, I have to say I find these kinds of breaks within the building of a narrative intriguing, how the events of our living—when we are writing or not-writing—get folded into the overall shape of a story. We smooth over lost time, try to close the distance between who we were then and who we are now. It's a novel onto itself. But let's get back to this novel. Is it helpful to start with that question I asked you when we first set out: How will you begin? Or is it more useful to ask: How will you return?

R: This reminds me of the question Xavière Gauthier asks Marguerite Duras in *Woman to Woman*, their book-length compilation of five interviews. Although perhaps it's more like: "How can one begin?" Do you know the video of an interview Muriel Spark gave, where someone asks her how she writes her books and she says, "First I write my name. No, first I write the title and then I write my name. And that's a book." I'm paraphrasing somewhat, but she does treat the question quite simply and I like that.

I: So . . . ?

R: Girl! I don't know.

I: Where is June inside the novel? I mean, where has she been all this time? Is she still in that bathroom about to take measurements?

R: I'm almost afraid to go and see. What if the book has vanished entirely in the time I've been away?

I: We're here . . . we're still talking. So, June is probably somewhere too.

R: Umm . . . that's a good perspective. Let's see.

I do my work. It ain't weird. Not when there's other people around you doing similar things. But there is some loneliness that comes with working in numbers. I've got to layout this for the seventh time and I've been here for hours. It's been dark for hours. My phone has been blowing up, but I haven't wanted to break my concentration to see what's going on. Something is stirring in me. Has been for weeks now, since Hudson. For months now, since London. And I'm no closer to understanding what's happening. Ellis says I'm a ferry moving full steam away from him and he's kicking himself because he should have noticed before I ended up in the middle of the sea. He says it's dark and the sea is churning from the ferry's engines, so he can't even see me anymore. "Where was I when you set sail," he keeps moaning but also leaving for work trips. I do my work. I make three tentative plans for the suspended porch. Marcel keeps trying to get me to go out with him. He thinks I'm obsessed with circles. I am in love with moons, spheres, but I don't tell him. I want something that is mine and none of it to be the fleeing stuff that seems to belong to me. I'm that woman who wakes up in a field of fragments. Half saying everything I'm thinking. I have said yes to one thing: accompanying Marcel to the Gego retrospective at the G.

When we go, it's a quiet afternoon. The show has been open for a couple of months and the city is hot and sleepy. Esther will meet us later for a coffee, but in the meantime, we are traversing the spiral, though at different speeds and on different levels. I am moving so slowly I'm not sure I've even begun taking the show in. I'm thinking about all the negative space in Gego's wire sculptures, everything unsaid. My phone buzzes with a message from Marcel:

Move your butt!

Followed by another:

For real. What's wrong? Why are you staring at the floor?

Me: I'm thinking about space like we're supposed to be doing.

"You're thinking about space?" *A low voice interrupts my search for the perfect emoji.*

"Did I say that out loud," I ask, turning to take in the intruder. For the moment, we have one of Gego's Square Reticulária *to ourselves.*

"You did, but I'm not disagreeing. Did you want to finish that?" She nods toward my phone. I add "smssshi" quickly and send the text, because I want Marcel to know that everything has changed. I turn back to this woman, trying to figure out how to tell the truth. "I have this feeling in me that every time I see you—" But then I stop. "Not sure how to complete that thought."

"So, you do remember me?" She looks less confident than she did a moment ago.

"It's not so much remembering as it is a stirring-up of strange weather when our paths cross. And I know the feeling comes from the past, but I can't grasp it."

The smirk is back. "Isn't that just an existential way of saying you don't remember?"

"Not when your moon is in Virgo."

"What happens when your moon is in Virgo?"

"You want order and, if it's not too much to ask, to hear that click of everything sliding into place."

Then her soft laugh is rolling through me.

"Do you want me to tell you how we know each other?"

"Not in this climate! I'm not sure I can handle it."

Smiling, she says, "Okay. I'll wait but I need to get your number or something."

"You're going to call me?"

"I'm going to text you and ask you to meet up for coffee."

"Are you British?"

"When I'm looking out a window or walking somewhere."

Now, it's my turn to smile, which I do shyly.

I: How did that feel? You look like you're turning something over.

R: Yeah, it's nothing to do with the story. I was just struck by something I got wrong in our conversation earlier that has kind of broken my brain.

I: What is it?

R: I get things wrong—dates wrong—when I'm telling stories from my life and, when I discover this, I have to decide whether to go back and fix the error I've made or incorporate having made the error into the story I'm telling.

—

I: Why would keeping the error be important?

R: A book I wrote in 2004—*TOAF*—memorializing a completed but failed novel I'd attempted in the late nineties begins with this problem: me not remembering whether it was 1999 or 1998 when I started the book. An urgent fact for a memorial, right? When did the thing you're building a monument for come into existence? After researching my journals from those years of living in San Francisco, writing that novel that was never to be, even though I had by all accounts finished it, I'd finally landed on what seemed irrefutable evidence that it was indeed 1998 when I'd started the book, not 1999. At the time, in 2004 when I uncovered this truth, I asked myself should I go back and fix this part of *TOAF*, where there is a lot of waffling about when I started the book and what I was eating at the time. But I couldn't because that uncertainty had become a part of the architecture of the memorial. More recently, when I was writing the lectures for *Theory for Moving Houses*, I found myself repeating this gesture. Changing my mind about something I'd written but allowing the correction to exist as an event in the writing, a part of the story of writing. I mean, I think that's why we're still doing this, talking about this book that is more desire than reality at this point, because the story of my writing it is almost more integral to my living than whatever *it* will or may become.

I: So what is your error with regard to this narrative?

R: Okay. I don't think I've said this yet, but I started a journal a couple of years ago that would tell the stories of my drawings, the ones I've sold or exhibited, so that in case I don't have images for them I can recall what they look like and when I made them. But, as you will likely suspect, I began to have some issues around when certain series of drawings were started and how I got to them from where I'd been previously or the materials I'd used for them. Specifically, I was wondering when I made my first black paper drawing. That required me going through my journals about eight years back then reading forward. In doing so, I stumbled across an entry from August of 2017. Before, I said that I'd started this novel, this one in which we are sitting, in the spring of 2018, but in fact I've realized that I started it in August of 2017. And that's completely mind blowing. 2017 felt like a very different year than one in which I would decide to write my own lesbian novel. Well, it was eight months into Trump's presidency, so I was probably looking for comfort all over the place. But if I had to give a chronology, I would have assumed that that first year I spent reeling, not venturing through new genres. So, how did I know to start this novel if I hadn't yet read any of those books I referenced earlier—the Alderman, the Grumbach? It would still be another full year before I discovered there existed a trove of lesbian romances, that lesbians had their own genre for romance and I wouldn't have to rely on these more mainstream disheartening novels or the ubiquitous, terribly written, poorly acted, cancer-ruining lesbian film. So, how did I get here? My dad died in 2017. I had my first art exhibition. I spent the winter in Marfa, TX. That was the year the Patriots were down 28 to 3 to the Falcons in the fourth quarter of the Superbowl and came back and beat them. I was so excited that I sprinted up the hill to where I was staying in Marfa, which I kept interrupting by stopping to dance, which I would have kept up for a lot longer had I not run into a family of javelina crossing the street, one wild pig at a time. 2017 was also the year that I injured my ankle so disastrously that I could barely walk for months. What else happened? I remember laying the drawings for *One Long Black Sentence* across many surfaces. Trying to see them essay. Essay in different spaces. We moved to the barn in 2017. *Houses* came out, as did *Prose Architectures*. . . . What's *your* memory of when we started this?

I: Oh! You're talking about the interview, too?

R: In my mind, there is little distinction.

I: Then I'm not sure I have the capacity to answer you.

R: What do you mean?

I: Well . . . if I were here when you began this novel, since I was the one asking you about it, wouldn't I have known you had the years mixed up? Although, I guess we both could have experienced the same lapse in memory. I'm just trying to avoid things getting awkward around what's inside the frame of the book and what's outside. . . . Do you think we just broke the fourth wall?

R: I'm not sure there was one to begin with. Did you do this when you were a kid? Knock something over by accident then slink away before anyone notices.

I: Oh! You want us to pretend we didn't just find this big glitch?

R: And be historically inaccurate?! No way.

I: Okay. So, let's move on. I have a question anyway about the novel that I should have asked pages ago. What's the British woman's name?

R: Umm . . . do I know?

I: Well, what did she type into June's phone?

R: I have no idea. I haven't checked yet. Honestly, I can't remember the name I dreamed up for her, and I can't find my notebook where I wrote out my first thoughts about the novel. There's the mention in my journal from 2017, but it's just me saying enthusiastically that I'm on page thirteen. Where the hell is the other notebook? I started the novel by hand in one journal and took notes in another? But not my normal journal where I wrote about writing? And not the journal where I exchange letters with Danielle? I just don't know what I was thinking. It's also very rare that I find an entry that precedes the opening of a new book, something that says, "I'm starting a new book today because . . ." I always wait until I'm some pages in before I reflect on my progress, and then years later I'm here wondering why I started the book in the first place and where the book is. Do you have this? Always wishing you would do the thing you're always wishing you would do? Where are *you* when you start your books?

I: I'm not a good reference. I've been writing the same book for the last twelve years. *Monuments.* It's basically a 600-page paragraph and has no characters, just place names and colors. If I ever finish and if anyone ever wants to know about its origins, I will just point to the first page, which documents its own inception.

R: Good thinking.

I: Only if I finish.

R: I'm sure you've finished several times.

I: It's true. Some things really aren't about finishing. They have no end! They traverse a circle as a circle. The only downfall is after a while you have no idea how to get out. I keep adding pages that further the curve. But . . . back to you. Is there any chance that you hadn't yet named this character, especially since she exists as a kind of fog for June?

R: I asked Danielle this morning if she thought it was like me to have started a separate journal about this lesbian novel, if I already had three dedicated spaces in which I could have written about it, and she said no quite confidently. She's usually right about these things, but there is this itch in my brain that there is a misplaced fourth space, a small, dedicated journal, which if I found it would tell me the name of this character. But, yes, there is a slip of a possibility that I hadn't named her yet.

I: And you still contend that these last pages that we've just lived through are not about a sort of loss or degradation of memory?

R: I *contend* that whatever my issues are with memory are completely different from what June is experiencing. They have to be. We are totally different ages! There's almost fifteen years between us.

I: Okay. Okay. Note to self: discover why Renee is so sensitive regarding her calamitous memory.

R: Ha ha. Are we done?

I: Not even close, dude. But we are at an impasse. So, what did the British woman write into June's phone?

—

R: Umm . . .

I: Can't you name her anything!? I mean, what is going on here?

R: For me, this is a pivotal moment. Reclaiming this memory is utterly essential. Determining whether it even is a memory—there's a small chance I was waiting to name her until she became a full presence in the novel, as if June needed to first understand the value of the British woman's existence before I allowed myself to see her fully, or it would be near simultaneous: June would know then I would know. But why didn't I write this out in one of my journals? I know! You think I'm obsessing. I tried to discuss this with friends the other night, I thought a riot was going to break out.

I: It's funny. I wouldn't have said this before but since we've been talking about tropes it struck me that you have a preferred trope. I was thinking it could be called "the uncertainty trope."

R: I can't really argue with that. I remember in school we used to talk about unreliable narrators, and I've always been drawn to them. I like to think they're unreliable not because they're dishonest but rather because they are paying attention to or, at worst, are afflicted by gaps in the memory of experience. These are characters that are most affected by the commotion in the field.

I: That's a term you talk about a lot . . .

R: Yes, I've referenced it countlessly, a concept I borrowed from Erin Manning and Brian Massumi in their book *Thought in the Act*. I really loved their idea of seeing space as commotional, as always in flux, shifting, responding to change. And I took it upon myself to see it as not only describing spaces where the body enters and traverses but also that of the sentence or paragraph. That of the drawing page and whatever abstract space encompasses subjectivity. You are unreliable because everywhere you go the *going* itself, and even more densely *having* gone—these are philosophical propositions. They aren't facts. They are dreams mixed with memories held inside questions with their windows blown out.

I: So you would admit that June is unreliable?

R: June is unreliable! Renee is unreliable! And probably you, too. Seriously, though, I like the idea of the uncertainty trope, but I have to push back against the idea that it's merely a device. I am often uncertain in my work because I do feel a need to pair fiction with some minor occurrences in my autobiography. Somebody—I don't know if it was Lyn Hejinian or Travis Ortiz, both co-editors of Atelos, which originally published *TOAF* in 2008—described *TOAF* as "a true account of a fictional story." This wasn't something we agreed upon; it just showed up as the main descriptor of the book, and I loved it.

I: Yeah, that's right up your alley in terms of ambiguity.

R: It is *everything* in a deeply delightful way.

I: Do you want to talk about it?

R: I do. But I also want to get back to the novel.

I: I find "delight" to be a very particular emotion to associate with . . . I don't know . . . what would you call it? A problem of time or category? Perhaps talk about that briefly and then we'll return to the book.

R: Samantha Hunt writes in *The Unwritten Book*, "Mishearing is how I love the world." I read that as a testament of delight, of play. I delight in living by misplacing information, by allowing minor occurrences or shifts in my daily life, or the daily life of some fictional aspect of me, to expand or spiral to the point of absurdity. So, you can imagine, after the mess of dates and walls we've just had to negotiate, I'm really enjoying life right now.

I: Definitely. But, back on topic. What *is* this bitch's name?

R: Hey, don't be rude! She's one of my heroines. Okay. Let me see . . .

We are all in high-stress mode with the Detroit House, everybody send-ing their numbers back and forth. It's shaping up, even though there's all this tension between the groups. It's probably a lot like filmmaking, so many different people you're depending on. I've been staring at these digital blueprints of the roof exchange for hours. Something is missing. It sort of feels like that everywhere. Ellis is always missing these days. In Singapore this week. Esther is on a research trip. Marcel is in the studio. I don't want to see anyone else, anyone new to whom I'd have to explain where I go in the middle of conversations, what I'm writing down and scratching out; even answering where Ellis is annoys me. I have no idea! He just keeps saying he's working and I'm at sea. I'm in my numbers, he also says. He's right, though. I'm in my numbers, trekking across this fungal landscape, trying to discern what's real and what's embellished. Looking through mushrooms at these presences in my past: Where are my feelings? Why is everything so full but my energy low, like I'm extinguished? I've stopped trying to categorize the mushrooms. Just wondering where my world will go from here.

A message chime pulls me out of my fungus. I know it's Griffin with the fifth reminder this morning of our meeting tomorrow, but I look anyway and lose my breath when I see it's not Griffin. It's the woman from London. I haven't heard from her since our run-in at the G ten days ago. I'd be lying if I said she hasn't been on my mind. She's been everywhere. On all my surfaces. What the hell?

> *Thena: Hi June. I wonder where you are on this gorgeous day. The humidity is low. A perfect day to sit somewhere and get to know a person. Are you free?*

—

Breathing is not more important than the stillness my body needs to keep my heart in my chest. My reaction to her text is completely unreasonable. A thrill overtakes my nervous system. Am I that lonely?

> *Me: How did you know I needed a reason to step away? I'm working but I could use a break.*

> *Thena: You want the truth or something more socially acceptable?*

> *Me: I don't even know how to respond to that.*

> *Thena: Come meet me. I'll send you a pin. East side or west?*

> *Me: West, uncrowded.*

> *Thena: Will do.*

Who is this woman? She is an absolute question mark. But one I seem to be moving toward—throwing shit in my bag, stuff I want to show her for some odd reason. Perhaps it's just the idea of meeting a new artist, one from a city whose architectural history goes back so much further than this one, a city with secret underground rivers—although it's true Manhattan has its own lost rivers. We don't often talk about what we can't see. Do I need someone to be other *with? Thena does something to my mushrooms when I bring her near them (for example, when I'm re-reading our text thread or just thinking her name, won-dering why she's here): they swell up as if after a heavy rain and they multiply.*

I find her an hour later on a flat rock perched over the Hudson.

"I was worried you weren't coming."

"I should have told you I live near Union Square."

"Oh. Oops."

"No. No big deal. I like to relocate."

"I like your sneakers," she says. "And your hair. That shirt. Your ear-rings. And your pocket protector."

"Uh . . ." Then I add privately to myself, "Uh . . ." I can't believe she noticed my protector.

"Sorry," she sort of chuckles and sighs at the same time. "I'm nervous."

"It's okay. Do your friendships usually begin so mercurially?"

She reaches out an arm and helps me up onto the rock. I'm so glad the heat's let up enough to let us be with the water like this. I wonder which of the rivers I should tell her about first.

"I'm not sure I've ever started a friendship with someone I've met before but who doesn't remember me."

"I do remember you, Thena. But when I reach for specifics, it's all weather: fog, wind, tumult." I'm breathless.

"Tell me something I need to know about you," she says with her gaze pointed at the water.

"Okay. I have a boyfriend. His name is Ellis. He's in finance and travels a lot. When we were in London, he worked all day and I walked the streets, saw as much art and architecture as I could."

"You're an artist?"

"I'm a builder."

"What do you build?"

"I build fragments, like special roofs and walls and thresholds."

And then as if the words had just reached her, "You have a boyfriend?"

"Yes . . . traveling . . . Ellis."

We sit with the quiet between us for a long while. I'm watching things come in and out of sight on the horizon.

"Tell me something else."

"When I was in London, something began to happen to my memory. That's why . . . I don't know. Do I seem pixelated to you?"

She turns to look at me. I hadn't really meant to invite study. I want to remember to ask her about her art. I see specks of paint on her knees. She's wearing cutoff shorts and a big linen shirt.

"I like your necklace," she says so quietly I am reading her lips more than hearing her voice.

"Will you tell me something?" I ask hesitantly because I'm not sure what I can handle knowing about this woman, especially regarding the obvious unspoken narrative between us: What happened in London, why does she bring on a weather system when near me? I said I wanted to know about her art, but it feels wrong to start there. I don't even know

her last name. She never answered as to whether she was British. She's very beautiful. Her voice is raspy but also proper. Then occasionally something else, something more street-level. I want to ask her a question that takes her a long time to answer, where she forgets she's speaking and starts using her hands. I don't know why. Maybe she's like a building to me. And then I realize she's already talking, and I've missed most of it.

". . . I could go up or lean over. It wouldn't matter to me," she finishes with something too bright to hold rushing toward me.

I: Well done.

R: Thank you.

I: How do you feel?

R: Like I need to stare up into the trees for a long time. That's how I think.

I: What do you need to think about?

R: For one, dialogue. How to write it, how to get it to do what I want it to do, how to understand what I want it to do. I'm just noticing all the decisions, choices I must make to get across what they're feeling: Is it okay to simply render June and Thena's speech or is it better to support their exchange with "I said" and "she said"; should I build an environment or choreography around their speaking with observations like "Thena turns to gaze at the water, returns her eyes to me" or "Thena looks as if she has more to say"? It's not as though I've never written narratives where characters talk to each other, but I don't think I've ever tried to approximate real communication in any previous book, where you're talking about your day because you want the other person to know what happened. And you're maybe even expecting follow-up questions. Speech has always been more of something flickering in an atmosphere for me, a way to give dimension to a space or event, a way to enclose a particular feeling. I can't overstate how different I perceive that use of speech to be from the way it's deployed in the romances I read. In romance, there is something deeply literal there, something brought over from real-life situations that I think is actually hard to achieve in real life, which is probably why there are romances in the first place. For example, a character in a romance is often more likely to catch fleeting emotions as they cross another's face. Sometimes the characters discuss these feelings; other times it's a secret between the narrator and the reader. But what I'm saying is that feeling itself, the experience of feeling, is attributed a kind of presence in romances that is almost phenomenological. That's probably too weighted of a word to use in this context but I can't think of an alternative. What I mean though is, for example, how embarrassment might suddenly appear within a narrative moment: the organic response in the romance is to extend this moment, observe all its nuances: a character stares at her hands folded in her lap; she blushes; she goes to speak and her voice cracks; tries again, utters some apologetic words. The other person reaches to console, offers encouragement, maybe experiences a swelling of warmth in their chest (that's usually the beginning of some love feeling) or they fail to meet the moment, change the subject. It's a whole drawn-out thing and nothing else matters until we get to the other side of it.

I guess what's giving me pause is my own ambivalence about what I'm doing here, writing a romance, which honestly is not dissimilar from my usual awkwardness with fiction in general. It's always been difficult to explain how world-building is a secondary, almost involuntary act when I'm writing prose. It sounds like I'm saying I don't care about the story that emerges or I'm not making decisions to send the story in one direction versus another. It's more that my care and my choices are engaged in something that resembles storytelling near perfectly but somehow isn't storytelling at all. But what I am sure about or what I wish to achieve is a kind of sublimation, and just now I was wondering how to achieve that through dialogue. How to say something deep enough, resonant enough that it brings on sublimation but also remains in the realm of communication.

I: You've said so much here that I want to explore further, but let's start with the last thing you mentioned. Sublimation is one of those words that I've never been sure about. Can you say more? What is sublimation in the context of the lesbian romance and whose are we speaking of—yours or June and Thena's?

R: It's foggy, but I'll try to make it clearer. I'm really drawn to this verb *to sublimate*, but I don't think it means what I want it to. The closest definition I've found is the chemical one indicating something changing from one form to another. But I also want to conjure a feeling of *going under* when I use the term, the way people describe hypnosis, as if you're being pulled to a different field of consciousness.

I: Who's being pulled under in this instance?

R: Everybody, in different ways, I guess. I am not a musician, so I can't say for sure. But hearing a jazz pianist or bassist improvise, for example, like Reggie Workman's extended bass solo on John Coltrane's *Olé*, or the entwining of Alice Coltrane's harp and Pharoah Sanders's sax on her *Journey in Satchidananda*. I mean, you can find this moment in every good jazz tune, a place where the instrumentalist *goes under*, crosses into freer territory, where the rules of what is and isn't, of what's inside and outside are malleable. Logic is malleable to a point. It has to maintain some core of rhythm, otherwise you get thrown out of the song, but its path follows a deeper math or awareness between groups of notes. This is probably a quality belonging to most forms of composition and improvisation. Not everyone is looking for it when they work, but I very much am. Even in this romance I'm trying to write. I want a porous field. And I want the porosity to be horizontal and vertical.

I: How would that work?

R: I see the horizontal plane as that of the sentences, the gathering paragraphs, and let's say above or below the plane of writing are various planes of experience and reflection for the writer. The vertical plane belongs to the world of the book, and it represents the space between characters or between fictional objects. If you drew it like the x and y axes you find in geometry, where these planes make a kind of cross shape when brought together, the porosity could be demonstrated by a dotted circle that crosses both axes, showing flow from the horizontal planes through the vertical ones—the ones you can see and the ones you can't. So, for me, to sublimate would be to ride that curving line through all these fields. The surprise is wanting to do that in this kind of story.

I: You mentioned at the very beginning of the interview that most of your work tends to have some romantic or sexual aspect to it, even if only minutely. Can you talk about how what you're doing here differs from what you've done before and how that difference impacts the language level?

R: I'm glad you brought that up again, because the first time you asked I was a novice in the romance realm, and, as I proclaimed earlier, now I'm a scholar. I'm being facetious when I say that, but I have read a thousand of these books since discovering them, so I know their textures and contours well. Did I say that a large majority of books in the lesbian romance genre are poorly written? This is the case for hetero and other queer romances, too. It's an asshole thing to say but no less true. The genre does not regard language as a living force, as an inhabitable space, a space for encounter. Rather, each sentence tends to be treated as if it were a sharp-edged container with one function. Like: point. Or: explain. Or: dramatize. It goes: "Lucy opened the refrigerator." "I drove home." "We looked at each other with heat in our eyes." "Doug nodded." "Bess was puzzled." "After everything that happened yesterday, Morgan knew what she needed to do." In a way, these are the sentences we live with. Maybe we don't say them, but this is what we're acting out all day, and someone had the bright idea, yes, let's use these sentences for writing. Conversely, though, literary fiction is bad with love. Very very bad. Like ugh, could this be any more devastating, any heavier or more hopeless? I do it too. I leave my characters sitting on hilltops for all eternity. I have them being swept out of a familiar world into an unknown and dangerous one. People walking the streets desperately alone, fleeing a crisis they can't even see. So . . . yeah . . . could I write something that made people feel good—women, I guess, or people who were excited to see women fall for each other—and could the language have some aliveness to it? Be porous? Be responsive? Make atmospheres?

I: How do you make atmospheres?

R: I want to answer that, but I also want to get at what's different between trying to write this romance and, say, writing the narrative of someone traversing a city with a shaky plan.

I: Or someone drawing so as to write? I'm not sure it's even fair to ask what's different.

R: What is it you want to know?

I: Umm . . . something like: What are you most looking forward to when you're writing? And whether that changed when you turned to this book?

R: Since I was a kid, I have always wanted to get further in, to get behind what's there. Or maybe push past the limits of how things operate on the surface. I remember that I used to pretend to teach the JCPenny's catalog to a room of invisible students, treating the product descriptions like codes. And, similar to when I'm talking about my love of numbers and equations in drawings, it never mattered what the something was. That was never where my imagination went. I was excited by the mystery I'd created by regarding the catalog that way. Writing approximates this experience. It allows me to create a space where things are maybe floating near or in front of their categorical belonging rather than being embedded within it. So, you're always seeing the thing in view of its displacement. I've never wanted to write a novel per se. I have wanted to inhabit the expanse of a novel, to *durate* within it, but I've never really wanted to do the plotting/plodding work to build one. I'd rather it be a largely empty space, a field with some nice shrubs and trees along the boundary.

This desire to write a lesbian romance was first recuperative, at least in my memory it was. Now I don't know because the whole timeline is screwed up. But I *can* say that for much of my adult life I'd been frustrated with people's visions of how stories of love between women should go. I hated, upon finishing a book or watching a movie, having to leave these characters I'd been traveling with alone or dead or still suffocating in marriages to men they didn't want. I'd had enough. I'm repeating myself.

I: Keep going.

R: Well, I still want to get further in, but I find that I want to stage something, too. I don't just want to see or invent; I also want to reproduce something nourishing for this particular moment of my living . . . well, a moment that has lasted thirty-four years now, which is the time of my queerness, ongoing obviously. It's hard to explain. No, it isn't really. I've said it already. Many times. But I wonder if it's too personal to put any plainer . . . I've always written about desire. And the body. And I've always wanted the bodies in my novels—those of my narrators—to encounter other bodies. However, at the time I started this book, I'd found, most likely due to the crisis we were living, that I needed any characters I encountered—by either reading them or writing them—to be in a safe place, at home and nourished, when I was no longer with them. . . . Ugh, my cheeks are burning.

I: Let me bring you back to a few minutes ago. You were going to talk about atmospheres. I'm interested in that but also in this idea of the novel as field or terrain. You said something about shrubs.

R: Right. I had to go away for a minute after that last exchange. I was kind of emptied out.

I: Where did you go?

R: We went to the woods.

I: You and Danielle?

R: Yep. We walked the fallen forest forest. It's our usual. Red trail to the yellow trail, break at the mouth of the blue trail—eat an apple, catch our breaths from the climb, swat flying things in the warmer months—then head back out to finish the yellow, then finish the red.

I: And I remember you said you don't see much as you hike. Did Danielle see anything?

R: Apparently, the forest floor is alive. There are verdant pools full of wood-frog eggs and salamander eggs. Purple violets. White violets. Wood betony. The skunk cabbage is huge. She stopped for a while to take a video of a fern I believe. Picked up something and filmed it from her hand. We checked each other for ticks at every stop. They're crazy this year. Found none. She told me to stop brushing against this one plant, which I hadn't consciously touched. I talked about our conversation. Feeling exposed, not knowing if I'm still telling the truth. It was a whole thing. I got to use my knife. Had to cut an opening into an orange so I could peel it. Drank water with basil leaves in it. Saw one large unidentifiable paw print. A couple of trees had fallen. What did you do?

I: I called someone I'd been thinking about and asked her if she'd meet me. It's not a date.

R: Oh okay.

I: Are you smirking?

R: No. Of course not.

I: Anyway, why do you call it "fallen forest forest"? I think you did that somewhere else.

R: Good memory. There is a river in Ravicka called the Fallen River River. I'll get back to that. Maybe. But I want to talk about novel space, and then I want to do some work on June and Thena.

I: Okay. Go for it.

R: Have you ever read Henry James's *The Ambassadors* or *The Golden Bowl*? Julio Cortázar's *62: A Model Kit*? I know you've read Woolf's *To the Lighthouse*. What about Jamaica Kincaid's *See Now Then*? Nathaniel Mackey's *From a Broken Bottle Traces of Perfume Still Emanate*? The moment of influence is when you realize that, although you're no longer reading one of these books—the language of the book having long moved through you—somehow the shape of the field which held the language remains, is somehow an imprint. And once I realized this had happened to me, I recognized that a part of me wanted to write novels that would resemble these emptied-out fields. That would be molded by the shape and value of things having been there that are now gone. Not so much about loss as about the relationship of the expanded field—that is, novel space—to a kind of resonating *no-longer-there-ness*.

I: Why these books in particular?

R: Because of their liminality and the lushness of their introspection.

I: But if you're not actually writing from their remnants, what constitutes the *no-longer-there-ness* in your novels?

R: That's a great question. Moreover, how does one start something new as if it's an emptied-out field of something other? Maybe we should fade to black here?

I: Ha. Okay. So, how is June?

R: I think it's early morning, a couple weeks since her meet-up with Thena:

I wake with my hands between my legs, humming with my eyes closed. Arousal is near constant these days and the landscape of my thinking is shredded and clumped with growths. It's easy to believe the two conditions are connected. I come. I cross a bridge into mushroom territory. I see myself walking along the river, the seam a narrow footpath. It's crowded with people happy the sun is out after many days of rain. I find comfort in the lushness—

Hmm. I wonder if you could ask something specific.

I: About June?

R: Yeah. Sometimes I struggle with re-entry.

I: Well, what are you interested in discovering at this point in her story?

R: Oh, that's generative. Okay . . . let me see:

I keep going to places for work and running into brown-skinned women drawing on walls. Keep looking for something in them. The question with the Detroit House is how to optimize the natural light while at the same time honoring the tree cover. We're lifting the roof to accommodate the horizon. We're going to make a light field. I'm standing in front of a brownstone on the Upper East Side and, through the second-floor window, I see someone slowly draw a line across the west-facing wall, using what looks like one of those old-school yellow no. 2 pencils and a large drafting triangle. Her face is so close to the wall, I wonder if she's writing rather than drawing. From this distance, I can't make out any details. It's just a really compelling image of a woman wearing a large white button-down shirt that hangs fashionably from her slender torso, with a yellow pencil in her brown hand, although I can't say precisely what I'm compelled to do. I don't generally draw what I see, though she's definitely worthy of a portrait. I wish I had the skill. We joke at work that we draw the future, but I've always been mystified by people who can form a present with their environment. Synthesize a space by pulling its contents through the mind and body then back out into the world. With my next assignment, I want to think about bodies working interiorly. A house for an artist, for a drawer of lines. A brown woman drawing lines on a wall cast in shadows and patterns that layer the room with movement, making furniture, stuff you don't have to worry about cleaning. I hope it's not an outline for a painting or mural. I want the lines to be the site, even if I can't see them from here. But is anyone documenting her choreography with the wall? And when she turns her body fully toward the window to identify the source of the pressure she feels emanating from the street, it's worthy of a photo. Is someone taking it? I wave, point behind her, then place my hand over my chest. She waves back, nods, smiles, then turns back to the wall. "We're on the third floor," someone yells at me from the door.

I have sightings, but also too many blurred encounters, am seeing as though reading from a lost notebook. Esther says it's my brain looking for a new form and do I want to meet for lunch this week. Have I read Sergio Pitol's The Art of Flight, *Syd Staiti's* Seldom Approaches. *People undergoing transformation, she says. Also, cities. Am I undergoing something? I will ask her at lunch. We are always unfolding, I remember reading. We are woodshed, maybe Sonny Rollins believed. My mind fills up with useful sayings that aren't so useful for people whose memories are . . . I don't remember. I think that's why people keep texting me to tell me where to go and when. Griffin and Josephine at work. Marcel often texts to say, "use the hb pencil I got you" or "see you at Jack Shainman" or "give Lucious a good spray." Marcel is engaged at all levels of my living. "Maybe Ellis will like this?" a text he's just sent accompanied by a photo I ignore. Oh, Ellis. It's not like I've forgotten. But, Ellis. Ellis is in London, without me this time. London. I want to remember more about when we were in London almost two years ago. Thena. It's not that I don't remember her. But I want to remember more.*

Now that she's on my mind, I can't help wondering if she needs coffee.

Thena: I'm almost done here. Want to meet downtown somewhere?

"*Love to*," *I write back.*

And then we go back and forth a bit about streets and neighborhoods and rosé. Heat. Sweatpants. Tiny shorts. By the time the debates are done, I have only fifteen minutes to get where I'm going. When I text, I must stop to do it right, which means, progress is slow. She says she'll be sitting outside.

I get this fluttery feeling in my belly when I see her. Mushrooms are weird. I think I'm doing that thing where I've misappropriated how good it should feel to see her. Sometimes I forget what the emotional output should be for a given interaction and my go-to is "you've loved this person your entire life." But usually that happens with people I've at least known for a long time. Why would a stranger do this to me? Well, not a stranger. Although, there is so much I don't know about Thena. She likes linen. That much is clear. And her thick red-brown hair is sculpted into French braids today. When she senses my approach, she jumps out of her chair and opens her arms, even though I'm not yet close enough to step into them. She waits and seems to forget a world is going on around her. I seem to have increased my pace almost as if I'm jogging. It hasn't been that long since we met, has it? There's that flooded volume again. Do I love her more than anything? Why have I pulled her against me like she's just solved my life's puzzle? We both seem to have forgotten who and where we are. She laughs and pulls back, eyes dazzling.

"Damn, I guess I missed you," she says.

I try to equal her in her sort of soft merriment, but I don't think I get there. Something sad crosses her face. I borrow from the recent past:

"I like your hair that way. Look at the light on your face. It's like I'm at a show. I like your shirt. I like your ring. This place is beautiful. Good choice." *My eyes roam all over her, then down at the table,* "I like your drawing. Is that a drawing you're making?"

And her brightness comes back through laughter, as if wind chimes are sounding underwater. Rumbling, ecstatic, long.

"I like your ring, too," *she says with a gentle smirk.*

"Oh! Thank you," *suddenly remembering my hands, wondering where they are, finding them wrapped around a water glass. On my right middle finger is an oblong circle, not quite oblong.* "It's based on a Hilma af Klint drawing."

"Gorgeous. You weren't wearing it at the rock. I would have noticed."

"I'd had to throw myself together that last time. I'm not even sure I was finished dressing before I headed out." *I wonder if I should continue.* "I'm not sure I've ever met anyone like you before."

Thena does that thing again with all the brightness in the universe, "You were definitely dressed."

That is all the banter either of us can take because from this point forward the tone of our exchange goes from yellow and orange to taupe.

High quality, still, but overall sedated. Although, it's hard to hide dimples and there are four between us.

A few hours later, I'm home and flipping the pages of the journal I recently started. There's an entry from three weeks ago that I don't recognize:

> *Night right now. Too quiet. Everybody was ensconced today, so I did this walk along the river. I wanted it to take the whole afternoon. Had to run into a wind shelter when a storm blew through. Stayed undercover for a long time. Had to undo some numbers I'd pulled together to answer Cristina's beam question. Had to undo the tangle of Ellis and me, acting like ghosts. "You are drifting," he's been saying. "I'm looking at you through binoculars." He's unhappy with the growing landscape. His face asking, "Why are you changing?" When I answer I try to start from within his metaphor. "It's wild out here," I may have said during one of these conversations. "We are drenched. Everything is wind and water." Really, it's a repeating dream. I don't know what he's saying in real life. There's too much travel and too many daydreams. I miss going to T's. Why did they close?*

I: I think this is the most emotional distance you've crossed in the novel.

R: I kept wanting to pull myself out of it, but I made myself stay. It's hard to write this way. To write wanting to say something. Or . . . rather, to write wanting to produce something in particular.

I: Like a certain mood?

R: Mood with consequences. June is not just thinking so as to think or so as to move; she's thinking to effect change, and she's both aware and unaware that she's doing it. She's walking around looking for something, seeing repeating images, but she's not ready to see what she's seeing. Everything is dream-like and fungal. Meanwhile, I'm writing a kind of mystery unto myself—

I keep pulling out Marguerite Duras books, mostly interviews but also these more obscure texts where she's reflecting on the making of a film or writing anecdotally about her companion Yann Andréa Steiner. I love the way she writes about the houses she's inhabited in her life, about the sea, about how her living leads to her writing, how she writes her films. I can no longer tolerate how she talks about her relationships with men. She seems too enamored with mistreatment. It's weird though. I don't know why I didn't see this before in the twenty years I've been reading her books. I'm not sure why it looks different now. I've been thinking about the times I taught her books to young women, and I'm berating myself over a recent memory. It was last summer. I was teaching my favorite text of hers, an essay-memoir piece called "Writing," and I remember I kept saying to this class of women and non-binary people: ignore this, ignore that, ignore what she says about men and love. Ignore her drinking, too. And what was left was this life-long dedication to writing and the sea, but you can't really teach like that, and, apparently, I can't read like that any longer either.

I don't even know why I took that detour. I guess I'm thinking about what it means to let an interview become a novel and to let one's talking about the making of one's work become fiction. And the delight that comes from regarding oneself as a mystery, a mystery protected by a vigilant writing practice. Taking space to write. Starting and finishing books. Having a story to tell for each one. Duras does this brilliantly but also complicatedly and, from the current vantage point, a bit insensitively with her obsession with cruel lovers—past and imagined.

I'm saying this because I have a stack of her books here, but I can't read them, not the way I used to. But when I open them, I feel instantly the gift of her dedication to her work . . . and the sea.

I: What else is in your stack? Do you always write with books next to you?

R: I don't usually have a stack of books on my writing table because that can sometimes look messy. However, since this is the first time

I'm reading literature in any sustained way since 2017, late 2016, I'm celebrating its return by building a tower of books next to me. I want to see how far it will rise before I have to make some changes. They are quirky books, some of which I'm reading, some I plan to read. I've already mentioned Samantha Hunt's *The Unwritten Book: An Investigation*. Steffani Jemison's *a rock a river a street* is in the tower. Martin Riker's *The Guest Lecture*; Eileen Myles's *For Now*; Julie Otsuka's *The Swimmers*; Barbara Chase-Riboud's letters to her mother, *I Always Knew*; Christina Hesselholdt's *Companions*; and Vanessa Onwuemezi's *Dark Neighbourhood*—these are all of the tower. Polina Barskova's *Living Pictures*. Kathryn Scanlan's *Aug 9—Fog*. Two books I shouldn't name because they appear on the other side of this fiction and should be allowed their proper life there. And lastly (minus said Duras interview books), a biography of a mathematician written by Siobhan Roberts. I have another stack of newly acquired art books that I wish to read, but I won't list them. Not right now. They're in another part of the room.

And then there is my Kindle, where my trove of romances is bundled. I never ever thought I would write a sentence like the previous one. In any case, I have hundreds of titles there that I've just finished reading, am reading, am soon to read.

I: And will you name some of them?

R: Yes, I want to do this. But maybe a little later. I've been working on something this morning:

"I don't remember remembering," I tell Esther over lunch some days later, "if that makes any sense. I just woke up drenched in sweat."

"And I bet smelling a little like your own kumquat," she teased.

"Ugh, E, be gentle, will you? This is an absolutely unacceptable response to . . . to . . . I don't even know what I'm responding to!" I open my camera and stare at my face.

"I'm just saying it's nice to wake up coming. That's the portal I'd choose for entering the day and often do choose."

"This is all just crazy."

Something bright crosses the horizon of the fungal landscape, briefly illuminating the growths, which are starting to look like high-rise structures, knotted and braiding, as they ascend, the tilt of the horizon line suggesting that the land behind the structures might curve. I want to go where there is curving. I want to be completely led through sentences. Every day I'm working on formulas for magnetism and the light field. Pushing energy through form and having the form trap the energy instead of letting it through. It doesn't want to change, to be altered by the flow, so resists by becoming rigid. But there is deep material awareness. That is, the concrete wall knows that within it is already the energy that leads to change. You can't have materiality without it. Somehow, it's the math that is most incapable of digesting this information, wrapping its mind around the introduction of "e" and "k" to the equation. "Vector," I keep thinking. "Vector, vector infinity."

I: I bet you're smiling.

R: It's true.

I: Tell me.

R: I love the word "vector," even more when it's "vector, vector." I'm smiling because I know I should research how architects talk about building, what the math actually is—in fact, I do have a book on mathematics in architecture, and I borrowed from it to write *Ana Patova*—but there are two issues with that. One, it is so much more enjoyable to make up my own math and two, were I to try and grasp how a real architectural equation works—what it's considering, the path it travels—I would be stumped for all eternity, because I don't understand math as presently configured, or presently represented, I should maybe say. But I love it so. And, more than likely, were I to place that in the novel, people would skip it anyway. Who wants to do math while they're reading a novel. Fictional math is much more pleasant.

I: But how do you love math if you don't understand it?

R: I love that the numbers and symbols represent something unseen and that there are actions with equations or formulas that make the unseen progress, moves it forward and through, while it adds or takes things away from it. It's another way of seeing the sentence, the inextricable narrative quality of it. My problem with actual math is that its abstraction and the kinds of objects or situations the abstraction represents or stands in for never point back to stuff I really care about. Except for chemistry or physics. I did well in Chemistry. But problem solving? It's never the crucial problems, like loneliness or gender dysphoria or the shape of desire or the impact of racism or retrieving the body from trauma—at least, not the kinds of math I've ever been exposed to. I would love a math that engaged all the various perplexities of the person. Not to solve them so much as give them an abstracted form, an abstracted individuation, like an "x" or a "y," that would allow one to move them around, see them from different angles. I guess that's what writing provides. We put ourselves, our questions in each word, each mark of punctuation, so that we can study and shape how we go. This is really unrelated, but also is sounding off in my mind right now: the opening lines of a video that Serpentine Gallery in London made of the artist Barbara Chase-Riboud talking about her sculptures. I mentioned her earlier as a resident in my tower of books. I believe this is a must see for all thinking creatures. You don't know what she's been asked, so that makes her response even more powerful. She's eighty-three and looking back over a lifelong practice of making sculpture, elegant, worldly black woman, who has always let herself be free, even though she was born in this country. After an opening shot of an extraordinary sculpture—I think from her Cleopatra series—she says, "For me, sculpture was never a hobby. Sculpture was something integral to life. Sculpture *was* a life, as a matter of fact." And then there's a break to indicate a shift is coming, like the conversation has moved forward, and she says this. I'm going to tell you, but you must go see for yourself. I hope that as long as the internet lives, this video does as well. She says: "I don't hang my skirts. I don't drape my skirts. I slap my bronze with my silk." Then shrugs magnificently. It's breathtaking. Please go watch it now.

I: Just did. Wow, what an incredible presence. I'm floored.

R: Me too. Every time I watch it.

I: I'm shaking my head. How did we get here?

R: I just thought the way she activates the words in that last sentence—I slap my bronze with my silk—demonstrates what I meant when I said, "We *put* ourselves." I don't think I've ever read something that so perfectly enacts that feeling of being a subject in language. And I love how what she's saying is immediately both literal, in the sense of describing a process of making, and figurative, signifying an act of power and control. And I know it sounds dramatic, but I am changed since seeing this video. Maybe only temporarily, as I move on from things quickly, but hopefully not. I think I needed her voice and the memory I have of her casual strength of self as part of my knowledge about the world.

I: I'm not sure I've ever heard you talk about another artist or writer this way. Are you also a fan of her work?

R: I don't know it very well. And sculpture is the most challenging of the arts for me, all that object-ness. But her charcoal and handwritten text drawings, which I've been slowly studying this past year, are phenomenal. I owe a thank you to someone for bringing these drawings to my attention, but, of course, I no longer remember to whom I owe it.

I: Oh yeah . . . you've got your fungal landscape blooming.

R: Hey! Shut it.

I: That was a sweet detour. Shall we go back to whatever it was June was doing before we ventured off or is there more you want to say about the mathematics of writing? Actually, ignore that. I'm going to make an executive decision here because suddenly I'm very curious: How far along are we in this novel, June's novel?

R: I've been thinking about something you said very early in our conversation. You were sort of wondering out loud how many scenes it takes to make a novel, like what would be the minimal number of scenes required. And you joked that maybe I only needed one. When I taught more regularly, I was really interested in the idea that a novel could be written in a sentence or a paragraph and loved to challenge students with that prompt with the caveat that the paragraph shouldn't be summary; it shouldn't be the summary of a novel you'll never write or you hope to write but the novel itself, one paragraph long. I was interested in the level of compression and scope needed to achieve this. I'm not necessarily thinking about compression in my lesbian novel as much as I'm trying to avoid writing things I don't want to write. I think the argument people make as to why "Mary opened the refrigerator door to remove the chicken that had been marinating all morning. She grabbed the dish with her hand and pulled it toward herself. She turned and placed it on the table and went back for the salad greens she'd pair with the meat"—such a detailed description of an action that's not only unimportant to what is happening in the story but is also very uninteresting because it's very easy to imagine those actions without them being serenaded to us. I mean, the one thing I can picture in my life is pulling shit out of the fridge. Sorry for the rant . . . what I'm trying to say is I think people justify that kind of narration by saying "I'm building the scene" or "This is backstory" or "I want to give you something to see." But I neither want to read these actions in other people's books nor write them in my own. If

I don't, though, my novel is ten or twenty pages long! So, how far along are we in the novel? There are things that are hard for me to do fictionally, things that bore me and feel unnecessary—what I've just described—and there are things that are hard but must be done. Like June and Ellis. I owe it to the novel to show the dissolving of that relationship, but having to do so feels like those days in middle school when I had to drag my soul out of bed to go do this horrendously asinine thing within this dubiously constructed frame, which, in this case, was childhood. I think Ellis and June have been treading for a long time, enjoying the strong familiarity they've built in their time together, loving the success of their story from the outside—how good they look together, how successful they are in their careers—but the mushrooms have obstructed June's access to that ongoing narrative. Everything just feels different. Ellis is not wrong when he says she's drifting away from him, and apparently has been for a long time, as he claims he needs binoculars to see her. He's a mover and shaker. His job is blah blah—did I say what he does earlier . . . a lawyer? Anyway, most of the time, he's got tunnel vision. In the past, though, June was always there when he came out. It's been a sedate and comforting love but has reached its end.

I: Will you enact the breakup in the novel?

R: Ugh. Do I have to?

I: We were always taught "Show, don't tell." Although I realize that the essence of what you're doing here is telling. We can't really get around that. But, yeah, what do you owe the novel?

R: Yeah, and to which novel do I owe it?

I: Hmmm.

II

Marcel, Esther, and I have been moving as a trio through this day; it's supposed to be a sad day—Ellis has left me to move to London, "To get out of this weather," he said, meaning my vicinity—and Marcel and Esther are taking me around on a "heart tour." I haven't told them it isn't necessary, mostly because I love hanging out when it's just the three of us, but I'm telling myself the truth: I feel fine. I am in my mushrooms. I don't know which shit is up and which is down; it's all contours and eddies. And some thrumming has taken up residence between my legs. But I can barely say that to myself, let alone confide it to them. I'm silent about all of it for now. We're looking at books and bags and bottles. "All the best Bs," Esther keeps proclaiming as we try to cross West 23rd Street arm in arm. "We need to add some other Bs," Marcel intervenes. "Like burgers and beaches." "We could drive to Fire Island in the morning," I offer. I would love to see the ocean. Am I still stuck on a boat out there? Are you still distant if there is no one saying you are? "Am I distant?" I ask my friends. "It really doesn't matter whether you are or not," Esther replies. "Nobody is doing any measuring today." "We're just chillin," Marcel adds.

"I wish I had a canvas bag from all my favorite galleries," he piles on
after a long silence between us three.

*It's a lazy summer afternoon. People look like they're loving the world—
arms out, legs out, some people thighs out, butt cheeks too. Heads up
and swiveling as if they've got their own film crew in tow. Nobody looks
as fungal as I feel, no horizontal landscapes pushing out the backs of
their heads, friends holding them up by the elbows. I should just tell
these two what's really going on. I don't like secrets and I don't want
to be a fortress. I don't want to lead them on a wild goose chase. Right
now, they think they are on another safari. I conjure as many analogies
as I can. Coming clean, though, will at least allow us to talk normally
to each other.*

"Y'all?" I pull from my roots.

"Yeah, baby?" "Yes?" they answer in unison.

"It really is less that I'm sad than that I'm deeply confused. Not confused. I don't like that word. Definitely not curious! I'm in some kind of
speculative situation. But it's not about Ellis, so we can stop avoiding all
things E."

"I can say Esther again?" Marcel asks. "I have not enjoyed calling
her 'Stir' today."

"No one has," she confesses.

"E is safe, B is safe. Everything is safe. Even when I say 'mushrooms,'
nothing particular happens."

"We should go find a cava somewhere."

"*Pink. Cava. Brut. I'm in.*" And I am. I want that minerality and for it to feel like I'm drinking light from roses.

Esther remembers that we were talking about something important. "June, what were you saying? You're not sad?"

"I'm saying I'm not exactly sad about Ellis. He spent so much of the last year telling me how far away I was while being physically far away himself that I have to dig deep for happier memories. But . . . I do feel like a failed landscaper. What am I doing?"

"Is this about the dreams?" Esther asks.

I'm embarrassed momentarily. I can't remember if I've told Marcel about my dreams or even that my time in London has been haunting me. But he's a young dad now, so he sort of picks and chooses which threads to follow and which to leave dangling. He's probably also thinking about Scar, his wife. Thinking about the objects in his studio. Maybe he feels some kind of way about Ellis—compassionate? Defensive? Do I need to think about how he's a man among us? I've rarely had to think that.

We have reached a point where walking and talking as a trio is no longer viable. Although I loved being sandwiched between them, they've had to let me go. I'm propped up against the concrete façade so I don't drift away. We're standing in front of a gallery on 26th. A troop of young beautiful people walk by. Bags, sunglasses, painted toes. They're each *on their phones, talking animatedly. I doubt to each other. They are happy, though! And have no questions about their interior matter, no concerning bulbous growths to hide or confess to, depending on their natures. Then I think about my friends, who have been supporting me all day. Marcel is my age, thirty-eight, but Esther is forty-three. Surely, she knows what's happening here. Surely, after all the books she's read, after all that talking she does year after year teaching, there must be some measurable damage or embellishment done to her memory.*

"Esther . . . you don't have any mushrooms? Any problem with . . . with mushrooms?" I don't know what else to call the phenomenon.

We don't say anything for the duration it takes us to arrive at V's. We find a table under some wild hanging plants. I'm not pushing Esther because I've never known her not to answer a question. She loves to think. She's gazing up at the sky. Marcel is making his way through cava and french fries. I am spending some quality time in and out of my body. (Is that what he means by drifting?)

"The thing you've got to understand," Esther finally begins, "is I'm just not interested in sex right now."

"This is not about sex," I'm quick to say, staring at the second head she's grown.

"Dude, this is all about sex," she exaggerates. "And I'm not interested in it. Not for me, anyway."

Marcel wonders aloud, "Why isn't she interested?"

"I need the right stick," she volunteers, "and I can't find it. So, I've stopped looking."

Marcel sputters, but before he can find his words, Esther turns to me: "Love, I just don't think you want the stick anymore. Not entirely sure you ever did."

Now I'm sputtering.

Esther leans back and takes a very self-satisfied sip of her pink light.

I: She's a character.

R: Indeed.

I: Is she based on someone you know, or does she represent a type of persona one needs for this kind of story?

R: Yeah, there's usually a character who knows more, who has access to the macro view and can steer the MC away from misadventure. I appreciate this presence in a romance because, as I said, I abhor communication drama—people misunderstanding each other, not being honest, not asking questions, acting out of fear. I hate all that shit.

I: But isn't that the bones of any kind of story?

R: I don't care I hate it. When people start acting stupid I usually stop reading. Those people aren't ready to be characters yet. You can't have just any figment be a character. They should have to pass a test.

I: I think the argument is that novels are a space for growth and transformation; we are on a journey with a protagonist, rooting for them to figure their world out, make good choices.

R: Nah.

I: That's your response? There's no way you're against transformation.

R: I am not. But there is a level of maturity a figment should have to achieve before sublimation—that word again. But that's the process, going from figment to character. You are both going under and emerging. It's the beginning or end of molting—either way, you're not supposed to be stupid when you start this journey, especially not if you're a protagonist in a romance. Okay, let me give you an example. I read this book some years ago; it was about a straight woman who is a born-again Christian dating a born-again man. He's annoying and controlling, so there's no way the reader feels any sympathy for him; we're there to see her find a more open love, but generally would like her to do that without cheating. Not a fan of cheating in romances. Anyway, I think she starts a new job and immediately begins to fall for her boss, who is an Ice Queen. But they have some kind of weird angry energy between them that already has my shackles . . . what is it that shackles do? They're up? In a twist? Is it hackles? Whatever it is, I'm already pretty sure I don't like these characters. There's also an age gap, although with both MCs being so immature this is a nonfactor. So, born-again lives with a roommate, someone she's been friends with for a long time, and the roommate likes to sleep around. Somehow, the roommate encounters her friend, the born-again, with the Ice Queen boss and sees there's something brewing between them. Are you with me?

I: Yes, I think so . . .

R: Good. Almost done. The promiscuous friend asks the born-again if she's interested in her boss, and, as in any romance, the born-again says no, but obviously she's lying. The Ice Queen is annoyed that the born-again is born again and straight. I actually don't remember her motivation for doing the horrendously stupid thing she's about to do. So she decides it's a good idea to seduce the promiscuous roommate, go back to the roommate's place, which she shares with the born-again, I remind you, instead of her own presumably luxury apartment, and have loud sex with the roommate, knowing that the person she's actually interested in can hear them. That's only the first of a series of unethical decisions these characters make. This book has an HEA, not that I made it that far, but who would care after having to live through this yuck. I know people enjoy this kind of drama, but I hate it. This was, though, the first time it occurred to me that not every character is ready to be in a book. And that when you're reading for comfort, you are somewhat vulnerable to the whims of any given author, to their own sense of ethics, their preference for or avoidance of misunderstandings or the three-quarters-way-through breakup. There is something about where I am in my life and how the world feels to me that I need to know where I'm going when I enter a book. I don't even watch TV anymore, other than certain episodes of *Columbo*. My heart can't take it. Everything is too devastating. I can't even watch sports in real time.

This doesn't mean I don't want to have an emotional experience; I just don't want to be wrung out because two people don't have enough respect for themselves and those around them to act bravely, or at least to feel remorse when they don't.

I have to cool down.

I: You obviously feel very strongly about this.

R: I do. I'm baffled by the world—real and imaginary.

I: Do you mind if I return to the book? June also seems baffled by the world. Can you talk about her sort of "readiness" to be a character?

R: You have it in your craw—your caw? How did all these weird words get pulled into everyday parlance—but, anyway, you're stuck on this fantasy that June and I are on parallel journeys. I don't know how to disabuse you of this.

I: It's really not important what I think. I mean, that's exactly what we've been talking about, right? How each reader brings her own everything to a book. Sometimes something passes from author to reader, sometimes there's overlap, but a lot of the time we're reading for what we need. That's why you hate detailed descriptions of ordinary action—it's not what you need. But I imagine there are plenty of people who take delight in how a given character moves through their home or places an order for takeout.

R: Is that why you keep trying to make this novel a story about my memory failing or my general overwhelm regarding the world and this expanse of my middle life? Incidentally, did you know that my very first book, which I wrote under the clever pseudonym Renee Glad, was called *The Middle Life*? It received honorable mention in a manuscript competition I entered in 1994 but was never published. I knew at the time I titled the book that I would arrive here one day—in my middle life—and would think how this definitely wasn't the middle life I was talking about all those years and lifetimes ago. But maybe I figured I'd be able to smile at my young self and appreciate the opportunity to place the two expanses next to one another.

I: What was the middle life then?

R: I had only the previous year, my senior year of college, been exposed to experimental poetry, and my favorite of the group of poets we read were those who wrote in sentences. These were Lyn Hejinian, Gertrude Stein, Mei-mei Berssenbrugge, and Rosmarie Waldrop. For me, their work bridged a gap between daily life and philosophy. I was sort of failing as a philosophy student or, rather, balking at the idea of philosophy being something that had already happened, that we were now studying as a history and through a particular canon. We weren't being invited or trained to be philosophers ourselves and that confused me. I was expecting my classes to be a laboratory of sorts, a laboratory for thought. As a young teen, when I thought about what I wanted to do, it was a lot of sitting around and thinking, looking at things and thinking. In any case, in my senior year I took this course called Open to Experiment, and it changed my life. It opened so many doors, I wasn't even in a building anymore. I read these women and felt deeply that they were philosophers: they were thinking about language and experience and time and memory and relation and doing so in alchemy with language, making language material, textured, electric. None of this was what I was thinking then. Then I thought: there is room for me in experimental poetry, room for all my identifiers and displacements. This first book I wrote—whose contents I can't even begin to recall, although I think there was a long poem called "Jarvey," which was a made-up word for a way of speaking or a way of talking about seeing that was my own, not a made-up language like Ravic but rather a diction that followed its own rules. I called this the "middle life" because I felt that thinking or asking questions about experience through language was liminal; it wasn't *outside* of something dominant. It was *between* something dominant and something unseen. This middle life, the one meant to refer to age, well there is nothing *middle* about it. It's all encompassing. But how in the hell did we get here?

I: I'd asked you about June's readiness to be a character and you took that to mean I was asking about your own readiness. But I wouldn't have asked you that. How could you speak of it?

R: We agreed not to talk about ourselves metafictionally!

I: Exactly. I am not interrogating this space; I'm interested in what you're thinking on the other side of this wall.

R: As June? *In* June?

I: No, as Renee, in Renee.

R: Yeah. No.

I: But isn't this an interview?

R: No! It's a novel. And we've got to get back to June. She's reached a pivotal moment.

I: She's a "failed landscaper."

R: Yep, she's nearly overrun with mushrooms.

I: Seriously, though, where are we with June?

R: You're going to think this is random, but I was reading this article at ESPN yesterday, about a running back who plays for one of the New York teams. He's waiting for a big contract, but the team is stalling for whatever reason. I'm thinking about it because someone was interviewing him about the negotiations, and these guys are so much in the spotlight, and I often wonder who teaches them how to answer questions; there is an unreasonable expectation of eloquence, they're expected to answer questions but are also pressured by their agents or teams not to give too much away—this is rhetoric; you normally have to go to graduate school to do this well—so they end up speaking in platitudes or clichés. That's really all digressive. I just want to share this moment where the running back is answering a question about how talks are going. He says, "I think at the end of the day, if you really break it down and look at it as a whole, there is no rush." That *if you really break it down and look at it as a whole* . . . oh man, I love that. I love the paradox of it and the underlining necessity. That's what we've got to do with June: break her down so we can see her whole.

Something about Thena makes me want to fall to my knees and take her sex into my mouth, even though I've never done that before. I want her to destroy my face with friction and wetness and whatever else she's got. I love the way her vulva gleams with arousal, and I just want to get inside—

I: Whoa! Whoa! Jesus Christ. Just hold up a moment. How did we get here?

R: Oh, too much?

I: I mean, what's going on? Is she dreaming?

R: Okay. Let me back up.

About a week after the "heart tour," I find the courage to message Thena. I haven't seen her in a couple of weeks, but she keeps showing up in my sentences. Mostly things I say to Esther; sometimes, though, she comes out at work. I'm as shocked as anyone when I say at this morning's meeting, "Thena would draw this line thusly." Part of my surprise is due to the authority of my tone—how is it I think I know what her lines would do? We haven't talked about her artwork as much as I've wanted and I've been too nervous to seek it out, and not because I'm worried it would be bad so much as I'm trying to stay away from things that might be signs or portals. I just don't need any revelations right now. Esther narrows her eyes when I say this, re-shapes her mouth so that it looks like she's sucking something sour. And she just says "Girl," a lot. I close my eyes tight and say, "No portals!" After her comment about the sticks—her sticks and my sticks—I'm wary of her proclamations, but I also have seen her almost every day since the tour, like I can't get enough of the threat that at any point her speech will become unruly. So far, she's just sucking lemons. The other reason for my shock is finding myself repeatedly speaking nonsensically to my colleagues. Even if I did know Thena's lines intimately, they don't belong in or near the Detroit House; it's a creative architecture, but it's still based on ninety-degree angles. There are no loops and stutters in architecture. But why do I think Thena's lines loop? I imagine the cello when I think of her drawing. Things being straight until they are rounded. The brown women I see drawing on walls—their lines are too horizontal for houses. They are too ongoing. Houses have to have breaks, especially city houses, and some verticality. Everyone's looking at me when, for the third time this week, I open my mouth and say "Thena." I don't even finish the statement anymore. Griffin texts me as everyone turns their attention back to the slideshow. "Take five, June. And by that I mean five hours." Then he texts the stars, then the half moon. Griffin is not my boss. But he does give me an idea. Instead of treating my brain like an intruder or a mutinous landscape, today—and today only—I've decided to read it literally. I look at it head-on and it's just covered in placards that read "Thena, Thena" and sometimes "THENA." So, I'm going to go with that: call Thena, text Thena, move toward Thena somehow. I choose to text.

Me: Hi. How is your world?

I've relocated to a café across from my office. It takes eleven minutes for her to respond to me.

Thena: Hey beautiful. Whatever it was, it isn't any longer.

Me: Are you working? Do you have a studio?

Why don't I know this? Have I asked her nothing about her art? I try to be patient. It's been forty-five seconds.

Thena: Not really. I'm a bit of a nomadic artist.

Then it strikes me hard. I don't know where she lives. I have forgotten that I met her in London, that she just showed up here. Is her stay in New York temporary? I realize I've spent too long working my way through this when she texts:

Thena: Wrong answer?

I'm on it.

Me: No, I've just realized that I don't know how long you'll be here.

Thena: In the city?

Me: Yeah.

Thena: That depends.

Me: On what?

Also, wait! Did she call me beautiful? I have to scroll up to check. Yes, it says, "Hey beautiful." Was she talking to me?

Me: It's June by the way.

Thena: LOL

Me: Well, I don't know. Maybe you haven't saved my number.

Thena: I have saved everything.

Okay. My brain shuts down momentarily. By the time it restarts, I've missed a few texts. She wants to meet up.

Me: I think I'm ready to hear about London.

I write this and am suddenly flush with heat.

Thena: Okay. We can do that, too.

Too? Did I miss something? I'm sure I did.

Thena: Come to me. I will cook you dinner.

And I sit there for a while kind of exploded.

Thena: Will you come to Brooklyn?

We make arrangements, after which I toss my phone in my bag, then I drop my bag to the floor, then I place my foot on top of it.

I: There's no way June's about to go to Thena's house and . . . what did you say, "Fall to her knees." It's too soon.

R: What's happened to this interview?

I: Sorry. It's just suddenly you're rushing, and I don't understand why.

R: Well, this is the time in the novel where the narrative begins to turn toward the finish. I mean, there's still some work to do, but once our protagonist starts to realize she can no longer contain her feelings the ball really gets rolling.

I: I get it. Plus, I'm very excited to learn what happened in London. But there are a couple of things I think we should discuss first.

R: Like what?

I: The body. I'm interested in the body of the writer, the reader, the characters at this juncture. You wrote in the novel just now that June was sitting "kind of exploded" for a while. I wonder if you could talk about ways in which the body stamps or shapes narrative time?

R: Okay . . .

I: Seriously. You don't think this is important?

R: No, it's good. It just sounds a bit theoretical. I don't know when the sex scene is coming or how extensive it will be, but you're right I should definitely talk about how the body is called to form in these narratives. But when I'm done we're heading to Thena's!

I: Fine. Are you planning to finish soon? I'm not sure I'm ready for that.

R: Motherfucker! Whose novel is this?

I: Go on . . .

R: This is me narrowing my eyes at you. And you're in luck because that is a common occurrence in the romances I read. You narrow to discern or to threaten, sometimes for snark or flirtation. There's a lot about the eyes in general. People's smiles not reaching their eyes. People's faces being unreadable but their eyes revealing. The eyes pool constantly. In lighter novels, there's a great deal of rolling of the eyes, which I like. June is probably constantly rolling her eyes at Esther. There's a great deal of sparkle. A lot of dilation of the pupils upon arousal. I like that, too. Blue eyes growing very very dark before sex. Brown eyes resembling melted chocolate, usually with gold flecks. Green eyes, hazel, gray, ice-blue. A lot of nearly black eyes when people are angry or murderous. They shutter closed. Conversely, eyes fill up when you're reading—your eyes, characters' eyes—threatening to overflow. When their eyes fill mine usually do as well. Emotion streaming down the face or hovering at the rim. Not many people wear glasses in romances. Did you know that? And I've only read one book where an MC wears contacts, and that was only in the beginning. She was hiding her identity. Most lesbian romances you'll encounter feature white women, so it's like I'm getting an extended education in how white women want and love and fight and communicate . . . fictionally? In these books, blushing is a kind of currency. Oh my god, there could be a catalog for the different kinds of blushes there are and upon which part of the upper body—the ears, cheeks, whole face, one ear, neck, chest—they blaze. The variations in color—fire-red blushing, deep red, rose, pink, dusty pink, purple. It's amazing. I have some small jealousy that my skin is too dark to communicate in this way. In any case, it's perfect for the genre. Blushing shows vulner-ability, conveys desire or withholding. And then we have the core.

I: Yes, kind of a fundamental concept for many things.

R: True, but cores burn brightest in lesbian romances. They are both the site and the measure of arousal in the body. When a character starts to experience desire, it's the core that lets them know it's real. When a character says "Touch me" or "Please" or "Don't stop," they mean there's a fire at the center of them. When a character says "Come for me" or "I'm coming," there's liquid in the core. Sometimes a lot. Sometimes, it's almost like they're molten. And often, as is the case with the eyes, the core can overflow. The core is this great place to go when you're looking for a generator; it's the root of power and is a repository.

Above the core is the stomach and within the stomach are butterflies. I'm not telling you anything you don't know. That's my point in much of what I've been saying: romances are built from ordinary life. There are butterflies and heat-sinkers, arrows, other disturbances that act as a kind of proximity alarm. Someone beautiful is looking at you. Something beautiful is about to happen. Someone you approve of has entered one of your erogenous zones. The butterflies say you are a person on a precipice. The next time June sees Thena she will experience these flutterings. It's hard to say whether she'll acknowledge them as such.

I: And what about Thena?

R: Good question. Clearly, in this novel, we only have access to June's perspective, and that's unusual for the genre. These days, authors use chapter breaks to shift point-of-view from one MC to the other. I find this particularly interesting when the book is written in first person, seeing which strategies the writer adopts, if any, to distinguish the voices. Mostly, people choose to place the name of the character whose perspective we're inhabiting at the start of the chapter. I thought about this a lot when I was working on the other unfinished lesbian romance I referenced earlier—*Every Winged Creature*. I noticed only after I was too far in to change course that, at times, I shifted perspective between my MCs paragraph to paragraph, which is probably a big no-no in the fiction rule book. And I can see how it should be because of how easily the reader could get confused. But I'd also be willing to argue that sometimes it brings the story closer. To be able to be inside each character's head as something intense is going down, that could be electrifying for story space. I also found it weird, the longer I thought about it, that we would just go on upholding certain rules of narrative even when so much about time, connection, identity, etc. is changing around us. Outside story space. But, especially in queer love stories, you've got to figure out placement of names and pronouns, so the reader can follow the volley. It's fascinating to me to think about the tendencies we uphold and why we uphold them. Mostly, we uphold them to avoid confusion. And I think that's interesting, too. But, in the case of my lesbian novel, it wasn't possible to have alternating perspectives. Thena has been holding a secret for most of the book— what happened in London—and had she been given a POV that tension would have dissolved immediately. And then there's June's mushrooms, which is what the book is really about: looking at how one makes space for the body as it rearranges itself. So, we sort of need to be nesting in her, in June. But I do regret not knowing more about Thena. Intuitively, though, she seems enamored with June and doesn't appear to be struggling with that fact. I would definitely expect her to experience heat-sinkers and flutters and the whole gamut as she prepares for her guest. Are we ready to head to Brooklyn?

I: Are you done with the body?

R: Hmm. I should probably say something about lips and nipples.

I: If you can do that without making me deeply uncomfortable, I'd appreciate it.

R: Sure. I'll be quick. I am enamored with nipples in a romance. They come in so many different colors. When the core starts to ignite, the nipples can get very hard. This is really beautiful to read: nipples pebbling under thin shirts, hot mouths on nipples, nipples being tugged softly or roughly pinched, nipples brushing against other nipples. This is a moment of sublimation for the reader, or if there was a term for when the book creates a fold, like where your body is overtaken. I wrote about this in *Theory for Moving Houses*: you read, and you get wet. I think I wrote "a little wet," but I was being circumspect. Wetness is something that could draw you in or pull you out of a story. It's a matter of debate, when people talk about the degree to which a character gets wet, whether it's fantasy or the author simply not understanding the contours of the experience. For example, I'll never forget this scene where these two women are having sex for the first time in the back of a limo. They are both "gushing" arousal, but they are also on their way to an event so they're wearing evening gowns and thongs. These thongs are filling up and the choreography is hot, but when they're done, they just get out of the car and go to the party. No way man. Can you imagine walking around in a soaking thong? And considering it's a thong, let's think about where all that liquid really is. It's probably in their shoes by now. I was convinced the author was male. I've read many more novels by this author; I'm only semi-convinced at this point. The other side of the argument is that romance is for fantasy: everybody being their wettest, hardest, prone to multiple orgasms, no triggers, all that good stuff. Everybody also has full lips, and they can tongue for hours without drooling into each other's mouths. That really blows me away. Lots of dueling tongues, massaging tongues and nobody needing to excuse themselves to vacate spit. If I kissed like that, I or the other person would drown. Honestly, I'm glad these women have full lips. I like when one or the other nips the bottom lip, either their own lip, in thought or hesitation, or their partner's, in hunger.

What keeps me coming back, even though aspects of the romance formula drive me crazy, is that the people who write these stories understand how beautiful women are. And there is no more perfect way this gets demonstrated than through the narration of the orgasm. How lovingly and with such great texture writers, even bad ones, describe this moment of surrender in one character or between two characters. Sometimes, there's more than two, but I'll save that description for another time. The back arches, the breath is held, the neck tilts back, the mouth opens, names are called out or moans erupt, screams, limbs shake, they seize up, sweat comes and covers, the core empties out; then bodies entwine, they start over or seek comfort; they rest, they grieve something or reach for something then start again or sleep. It's like a poem or a long paragraph or a drawing. An unfolding, folding line. Some of them go and go.

After an uneventful ride to Brooklyn, I'm dropped off at a well-cared-for brownstone in Fort Greene. I can't believe how nervous I am. It's just dinner and maybe a weird conversation about London. Actually, that is scary. Who knows what she's going to tell me? It must be bad if I've blocked it from my memory. Yet, it's never felt that way, as if she held information that would destroy me or destroy our connection. It's felt more ceremonial, like I will receive this thing once I've completed my last rite. No, that's a bit heavy-handed. The thing she's holding, the way she's holding it, feels lighter than that, like she's holding a cloud for me. Ugh, that's cheesy. Why can't I figure out how I feel about this mystery? I feel okay about her holding it, that's the first thing. I feel safe because she's got it and no one else, which is weird since I still don't know her last name. Or how long she's staying or whether her lines "cello." Does she have roommates? Siblings? Is her family Caribbean? How did she end up British? Did she? I just know what her patience feels like: a warm bath, a cup of tea, a flannel. Ugh. What am I saying? Should I have talked to Esther before I came over?

A vibration from somewhere inside my clothes pulls me out of my weird spiral.

> *Thena: Hey! Been waiting for you to ring the buzzer. I'm coming to get you.*

My body lifts off the ground from an exploded circuit board. Rather, my brain lifts out of my body and the rest of me continues standing there. My mushrooms are glowing in the field. I just need to find some equilibrium, so I can breathe and be a person and be whole.

I land back in myself when the door opens and my body is pulled into a warm embrace, and something is dropped into my pocket. I already know what it is. If patience was made material, what would it be? A smooth rose quartz, I would guess.

"You okay?" *Thena's voice is husky with her welcome.* "You were out here for so long I was worried you weren't staying."

"I just suddenly had to think about everything at once," *I say.* "This building is gorgeous. Was it renovated recently?"

"I'm not sure. It's a sublet. Or more like a house swap. But we can talk about that later, yeah? Please come in."

As soon as we enter and I offer the bottle of Sancerre I brought, I ask her to show me the things that are hers. The first thing she points to is a healthy looking medium-sized jade plant in a clay pot. "This is Rita," *she says with her chest puffed out,* "I bought her the day after I arrived in the city. We are very close."

"How long have you been here?" *Another thing I should know but don't.*

"About a year," *she answers and walks across the room to a drafting table, sitting to the right of the front windows.* "The woman who lives here is an architect, so the table is hers. But this is mine."

She's holding a round metallic object in her hand.

"What is that?"

I didn't think she could get any brighter than when she'd introduced Rita, but she's outdoing herself now. I blink and grow warm where I shouldn't. It's just . . . Thena is very beautiful. You don't expect someone to open and glow and smolder and effuse and demure all at once. Her hair is nearly as thick as mine but redder, elaborately braided, whereas mine is all poofed out. Her eyes are green-brown. Red-brown hair, green-brown eyes. I wonder where her parents are from. She drops the object in my hand.

"It's my circle guide. A gift from my mum."

"It's stunning." Solid gold, heavy. "You like circles?"

"I do. And spheres. Planets. Marbles. Frisbees. There's one last thing I want to show you in this room. Anything after that will require a deeper intimacy. Cool?"

Cool that she can't show me more or that we're going to get more intimate? What are the things I'm supposed to be thinking right now? She grabs my hand and walks me to another part of the room.

"And this is Chuba, my French horn. It's a long story but, yeah, I grew up in orchestras. First following my parents, then in my own youth orchestras. London. Tokyo. Berlin."

"That's incredible. Why don't you play anymore?"

"I play for myself on Sunday mornings. The French horn can surprise you in its quiet: it makes quiet cracks within space, tiny temporary burrows full of even tinier daybeds. I try to open enough cracks to last the week."

—

She's looking at Chuba like they're the very best of friends; and I'm beg-ging space to show me how to be a quiet crack.

When she returns her eyes to me, they're shining:

"Something incredible happened to me when I was twenty. I'd sprained a couple of my fingers from a ridiculous and unfortunate fall and had to take some weeks off from touring. I was on my own in London walk-ing around, trying to clear my head. It was strange to be in one place for longer than a couple of days without meetings and practices. I'd had to put everything concerning playing on hold. On this day, I'd had this weird feeling that I needed to see time differently, see it performed or studied in some microscopic way, not just something that is constantly and furiously consumed or consuming. I thought a really slow movie would be a good place to start. I wasn't a film expert, but I was aware of certain trends in filmmaking that treated time itself as a character, the moving within and between frames. I remember someone mentioning Béla Tarr, a Hungarian filmmaker, in relation to slow time. And, also, Japanese filmmaker Ozu. Nothing of theirs was on at the moment, but I decided to walk in the direction of what was then the NFT, National Film Theatre, where films like these usually played. It was a long day of walking that eventually led to a place near the south bank of the Thames, where I sat and held my fingers. I couldn't believe I'd put myself in that situation—it was such a simple thing of tripping and using my

hands to catch my weight, but it knocked me out for weeks. So, yeah, I was sitting there at this convergence of the music I'd been playing for most of my life, the slowness of time I was desiring, and suddenly this line, double line of water extending before me. I wanted a life of these three things."

It takes me a moment to realize she's no longer speaking. She's leaning against the wall with her eyes closed, having already placed Chuba back in her case. Looking at her stand there in her silence turns something over in my mind. Something turns over, then vanishes or recedes. Something I need to see. Then I realize my eyes are closed: I open them to find a dark olive gaze on me. "Thank you for sharing that with me, Thena," I say quietly, trying not to break whatever this mood is that I would love to build a monument for. Thena—standing in front of her, receiving her gaze, looking at her face, the slight frown between her eyebrows— she has me somewhere I've never been before. "And that was when you stopped playing music?"

"That was when I started drawing it." And everything goes bright for the 700th time in her presence. Her smile is soft and coy. "Come on, June, let me feed you."

Everything is close but also light between us. Thena walks me into a gorgeous kitchen. It's obvious the architect loves to cook. It's not just professional and shiny but lived in. I don't know how I hadn't noticed the fragrance of coconut curry that's been simmering on the stove. My mouth is watering.

"I just want to give the rice another minute or two to steam. We're having halibut in a green Thai coconut curry. Does that sound good to you?"

"It sounds amazing. Can I pour you a glass of wine?"

She looks up from chopping cilantro and nods toward the cabinet near me. "Glasses are in there."

"Do you mind if I watch you?" I ask after pouring us both tastes of one of my favorite dry whites. I didn't mean the question as a provocation, but it does land somewhat salaciously. She stops chopping and her eyes are dark and hard for a flash before returning to normal. "I . . . I like watching people handle objects," I say. "That's all. It's one of my things. Salud." We clink.

"You like hands?"

"I like hands, bodies, and material resonances in space, yeah."

Okay. My little boat is drifting a bit too far from the shore. Out at sea, I say to myself as if I'm dictating a letter. Dear Thena, I'm out at sea. But even though I don't know her well, I know I'm not in danger. I just want more. I want to be closer. I want to be able to say what I'm feeling.

"June, you are something," she says softly and with dimples. "You can watch me if I can watch you."

"As long as you don't cut yourself."

And the next five minutes traverse through her humming and me being still, then Thena arranging things of beauty on a serving board, looking at me out of the corner of her eyes, my eyes riveted on this living, breathing architecture.

"Okay!" she says to conclude our strange activity. "Let's sit and break bread."

We carry our plates and glasses to a sweet nook in the room off the kitchen, where candles are lit. She thanks me again for coming and I thank her for preparing food, we settle into eating.

"Mmmm." I can't stop the moan from escaping. "My god this is good."

"Glad you like it," she says with a shy smile. "You seem like someone who'd love coconut milk and spices."

"I do. But I like a lot of foods. I have a very loving palate."

"Oh. Good to know."

We eat for a few minutes in companionable silence. I've stopped asking myself what I'm doing here, but there's a new question I can't make out.

"Thena?" I ask with some hesitation.

"Yeah? Everything okay?"

"I want to see your work."

"I want to see yours, too."

I hadn't expected her to say that. People don't usually ask about my work because it's so fragmented. I design thresholds and knobs and caverns. Her interest relaxes me. This feeling of home grows bigger.

"Well, my latest piece is a suspended roof in Detroit."

"Oooh. Road trip."

And bigger.

After dinner and a couple glasses of wine, I think I'm ready to broach the topic of my fungal landscape. I'm pretty sure I haven't told her about the mushrooms, and she should know if we're going to get close. She needs to know my memories are mutant mycelial hills. That everything important I reach for in my mind is contoured and gauzy and spongy. The mutations blister the emotions, so every feeling is high-pitched. But she's probably noticed that already. My eyes tearing up every other second. Gasping when she touches me accidentally. Incidentally. When I try to remember how we met by using my own crumbs. I was there, too, right? These memories are mine as much as hers. And before tonight becomes a warped field, I want to add this part of transparency. Showing her who I am. It's just I don't know exactly what that means. Will I say, "Hey, my thinking ground is fungal"? Or will I be more detailed? Starting with, "Whenever I go to think about how I know you, the ter-

rain of my interior, which is like a sentence, doubles, and the one that is the original hides inside itself, so it's still true but with a greater magnitude, which would be fine had this not happened hundreds of times at this point: me doubling every time I think how I know you, how we met." But I don't want to risk getting kicked out. I want to stay with her all night.

A hand lands softly on my thigh. It's like being brought back from a terrifying journey. We're sitting on a loveseat in the front room and, although the temperature is perfectly mild, I am trembling. Did I confess something? I don't know where we are in the conversation. That hand gently squeezes my thigh.

Thena asks me, "Hey. Are you alright?"
"Did I say something stupid?"
"You haven't said anything at all."
"Oh sorry. What were you saying?"
"I wasn't saying anything either. We were just sitting here, digesting, and watching the tiny flames from these candles sway. I was maybe going to begin to talk about London if you're still open to hearing the story. It's really not that big of a deal." The longer she goes on the less confident she sounds.

I want to touch her in some way that would be reassuring, like maybe try that hand on the thigh business, but then my heart starts pounding that I'm not ready. So, instead, I ask, "Why isn't it a big deal?"

"*I just mean, it may have been more important for me than it was for you.*"

I decide I need to be more honest with her. "*Even though I've had trouble remembering a lot from that trip, I assure you I'm fully aware of the magnitude of your importance to whatever is eluding me. And I promise that my not-knowing has almost completely reconfigured my interior. Not to be too dramatic about it all.*" And something in the quiet open way she's looking at me makes it possible for me to smile.

"*Okay,*" she sighs and relaxes into the loveseat. "*We're on the same page.*"

"*We are. So . . . let's go!*"

"*Alright,*" Thena's laughing now, a husky sound. "*It's a simple story, really.*"

"*Good,*" I say with some poorly disguised impatience. "*Tell it.*"

"*Fine. But you have to know that by the time I was five I was expected to be an adult. I traveled a lot with my parents, but I didn't see them per se. They had practices and performances, and they wanted me to meet with my instructors while they were with the group, the orchestra. Everyone was kind but also busy, so I had to get myself to a lot of places on my own and manage a shite ton of confusion alone. Sometimes there were other kids around, and once I started traveling with my own youth orchestras, things sort of settled in place. It was easier to understand what to do and how to be. All of that is to say I never expect too much from others. I don't expect them to be mean or callous . . . I guess I'm saying I have felt largely invisible. Even when I played,*" *because I was never a soloist. Well, that brings me to one bright day in Kensington Gardens, where I've just visited Serpentine—do you know that gallery? It's a beautiful space in the middle of the park that often has really special exhibitions like an Emma Kunz or Hilma af Klint retrospective, usually before other museums have the wherewithal to hold them. In any case, I'd just come out of the show and was walking around looking for a patch of grass to hang out for a while. These are rare days in London, where the sun is bright and the sky is clear of clouds. I found an area that wasn't too crowded and claimed my spot, lay there thinking about what I'd seen, and I guess I grew drowsy because the next thing I knew I was opening my eyes. It was very noisy around me like someone had decided to make me a center point for their party. I couldn't believe I'd let myself sleep for so long. And I couldn't help feeling vulnerable. What had people thought as they set up shop around me? And then something extremely beautiful happened. I noticed a stillness near me, and when I looked to see what it was, a gorgeous brown woman was sitting on the grass about three feet from me with a book in her lap; she was so close that had I brought a blanket with me, she'd be sitting on it. She hadn't noticed I was awake, was just sitting there, book forgotten, looking rather aggressively at the people frolicking around us. I wanted to know what was going on but didn't want to startle her, so I squirmed a little bit then said hi. Oh, she was shy and not at all prepared for me to ever become an animated presence. She immediately stood up, said sorry. I stood up too, somewhat dizzily, and asked her to stay. Showed her these dimples, then met hers. We sat again and I asked her what* had happened. She said she'd seen me sleeping alone in the field and got nervous when this large group of people started setting up around me, so she came over and sat to—and I quote—'make sure nobody did nothing stupid.' It sounds like nothing when I tell it, but no one had ever shown me that before—that I needed to be protected."

I'm stunned. I don't know where this story is going. But my chest clenches when Thena quickly swipes at her eye. She's upset and I feel like a robot, but I'm also furious at the people who didn't instill in her a faith that she's worth looking after.

"I'm sorry, Thena."

She shakes her head and blows my eyes out again with that my-face-is-literally-the-sun look, "Point is, June. Do you know who that woman was?"

I gasp because I forgot this was the story of our origins.

"Oh my god! That was me?"

"It was, and I have no idea why you don't remember it. Well . . . actually, now that I know a little more about you, I do have an inkling."

"You do?" I ask with my temperature rising. I'm not sure I can walk any farther down this path tonight.

"I can see you may have already reached your fill."

"I guess I just wish I knew what you were going to say so that I could process it before I heard it," I say and must immediately laugh at myself. She doesn't laugh but she does briefly reach her tongue out to touch her top lip. And now I'm binge watching some show, waiting for the next *episode to load. I have never felt before that I wanted to suck someone's tongue. As much as I've boasted with Esther about what I can do with my mouth—mainly to get a rise out of her but also because I'm proud of my talents—I'm suddenly realizing that if Thena lets me touch her with my mouth, I will most likely feel that I've never used my mouth before.*

It surprises me when she says, "You stared at me like that the day we met, sitting there in the grass." She's got that bright dark look.

I say, utterly flabbergasted, "I just don't understand why I would have done that. I was there with Ellis and we—ah damn I said something just totally inappropriate that day, didn't I?"

"You said you were hungry," she tilts her head as if investigating her memory, although it's obvious she closed that case a long time ago.

"Shit."

"You said I smelled good."

"Double shit."

"And you did one last thing."

"Come on! How am I supposed to believe this when I can't find a trace of it in my memory?"

"Can we try something?"

"Maybe."

"I just wonder what would happen if you were to repeat what you did that day."

"How crazy was it?"

"Not too bad. Just . . . lean toward me . . . closer . . . put your mouth and nose against my neck and inhale deeply."

—

I do it because I was already doing it. Somewhere in me I'd already decided to do whatever she told me to do, and not only because all my senses were gathered around the question of "What would it be like?" but also because I was still thinking "She should know she's worth protecting." But what would it be like to smell her? What would it be like to anything in relation to this person? "Fuck," I hear myself saying. I must have done what she asked and breathed her in. I open my eyes and all I see is beautiful brown skin. "Fuck, Thena. You do smell good." And then I remember sitting in the grass a lifetime ago and moaning in the neck of a stranger and remember how embarrassed I was after doing so. I was completely shocked and so turned on my panties were wet. It was too much to be feeling at once, alone in a foreign city, with a woman of all species. I can't say I've never found women beautiful because I have only done that. But I don't recall ever feeling this toward a woman. An absolute, all-encompassing desire to take her into me entirely. "Did . . . did I flee?" My shame is overwhelming. Am I about to flee again? Then something otherworldly rents the air. She's . . . I don't know . . . giggling. It's like a laugh being pulled through a blush. Ugh. What am I saying? Oh wait, now it's changing. It's a laugh being pulled through something molten. Sultry and dark.

"No, baby, you didn't flee."

"Fuck." *I almost come on her loveseat.*

We sit there a moment. I think she's giving me time to regroup. I say, "So, what did I do?"

"*Something that made me want to know you forever. You started drawing. I laid back down, and you drew something that looked like a grid in flight. I told you I was an artist, too. You corrected me and said you were an architect, which would have been my undoing if I weren't already undone. Then the party engulfing us got too rowdy and we had to jump up quickly and move. We shook hands but didn't let go. You were stunning and flushed. You told me your name. Said you live in New York. Said if I'm ever there . . . to find you. I said I would. You let my hand go, stepped back, and waved, turned, walked off. I sat back down immediately. Now on the edge of everything going on, and that's where I've been until this moment.*"

There were all these places where I wondered if I should drop out and return to you. I knew you'd have questions, but I couldn't bring myself to leave.

I: Hello, by the way. It feels like it's been a long time. So, what finally brought you out?

R: I needed to think about what I wanted to do next and couldn't do it there with June and Thena. I'm at a crossroads. If this were the formulaic romance, June would have in fact fled. That scene would be over; she'd be running her ass back to Manhattan. Thena would be left crushed and staring into the ruins of her whole crazy plan for making a future with June. We'd have to start over again in a way, build back that amazing connection they had before June got scared. Esther would have to intervene, calm June down, even though she doesn't know Thena yet. She'd be operating on a feeling that Thena is good for June because she's never seen June so emotionally awake. If this was one of those truly punishing romances, Thena would start making plans to return to London, too devastated to remain in New York any longer. And June, taking the time to figure out what she's scared of, avoiding Thena's text messages and phone calls, will be unaware that Thena has left the country. Then the day comes where shit finally clicks; she realizes her mistake in freezing Thena out, rushes back to the Brooklyn brownstone to apologize, to get the kiss she's been longing for, but when she rings the buzzer, it's the architect who answers the door. No more Thena. She's gone. June would have to get on a plane and get her back. It would be weeks, maybe months—for one author I'm thinking of in particular it would definitely be a year.

But, as we used to say when I was a teenager, "Ooh uhn-uhn!" We are not doing that.

I: So, what *are* we doing?

R: I don't know, because, admittedly, it didn't feel right to turn the heat up any further in that scene. June had definitely reached her outer limits. Thena kind of broke her brain calling her baby.

I: How does the scene end?

R: Thena's intuitive. She doesn't want June to leave but she won't push her any further, so I'd guess she asks her to stay and watch a movie. Oh! Now maybe I can enact one of my favorite events in a love story. Remind me—when I return—to give you a list of some stock scenes that are must-haves in a good romance.

I'm inside one of those clubs I've longed to attend most of my adult life, the ones you wouldn't know about unless you went out every night, knew everybody, were an extrovert, exceptionally trendy and a magnet, probably have to love cocaine or something. I am none of those things but still I'm in this dark place, the bass is deep and slow and sexy. I feel naked and elastic, and I'm doing my best moves, working down to the floor on a screw, flexing, showing off my quads, and the beat gets louder, the wall gets softer. I've got my drink in my hand; it's soft, too. Oh. That's not right. I stop moving, stop grinding the wall. The beat remains, but everything else club-like dissolves. This is Thena's body, and I've fallen asleep on top of it. We're on a wide leather sofa, having relocated there to watch a movie. I'm not sure I made it past the opening credits because I can't even remember which movie we'd chosen nor how Thena came to be lying with her back against the arm of the sofa, legs stretched out toward the other end, open, and me lying between them. But god it was a beautiful sleep. She seems to be at her own club because the grip of her arms around me has grown tighter, possessive, binding. My head is still resting against her chest, in the space between her small breasts. I can't help but think they are like mushrooms.

"*Mmhhhm.*" *She stretches and tightens.* "*What time is it?*"

"*No clue,*" *I answer. Then yank myself up to my feet when I realize my hand is on naked skin under her T-shirt.* "*S-sorry.*" *It's too dark in the room to read her face. So, I wait. Tension in the room is thick.*

"*Come here, June.*"

Aren't we supposed to be getting up, making distance? I stay where I am.

"*Come here.*"

She hasn't moved. Her legs are still stretched out and open, one arm along the back of the couch. I can't find her other hand.

"*Please come,*" *she whispers.*

Her "*please*" *is the end of me.*

"*You want me back where I was?*"

"*I do.*"

"*On top of you?*"

"*Yeah.*" *Her voice husky with sleep and darkness.*

"*Okay.*" *I lower my body back to that crevice she'd made for it. And can't stop the small moan I make when my belly touches hers. When my weight is fully on her, she turns us so that my back is against the couch, she facing me.*

"*Thank you for not running,*" *she murmurs and touches her forehead to mine.*

"*Okay,*" *I rasp out. I don't know what else to say. Her body is pressed against me. My brain is not exactly churning. I know what I want but I have no idea how to ask for it. I have never asked for this in my life. But it's the only way forward.*

"*Thena?*"

"*Yes.*"

"*But I haven't even asked you.*"

"*Yes, to anything . . . for you.*"

She's making it easy, so I don't have to ask. I can just do . . . become, and never have to say it. I could see what I think, then reverse course if I don't like it. She's letting me be reckless with her. I don't accept that.

"*Can I touch you?*" *I find oxygen in some lost corner of my body. A pulse in her belly jumps.* "*I want to touch you.*" *I have also found some confidence. Our mouths are close, but I want to wait before they meet. I feel pulled to that groove in her chest and bring my hand up from wherever it's been. My fingers tremble as I lay them against her breastbone. Her breath quickens. I see her throat swallow. I pull the V of her thin T-shirt down until one of her breasts pops out, and my mouth waters.* "*You are gorgeous.*" *It's hard for me to believe what this woman can pull off, probably most women, now that I'm thinking about it. It's so much power and vulnerability. Soon she's going to open her legs to me at the same time that she's looking me in my eyes, her gaze soft and intelligent, like maybe she's preparing me for drawing: she's thinking and inviting, surrendering and entrancing. Is this how we are? How have I not wanted this for myself all this time? But the breast has been revealed and I'm circling her aureole, the deep brown crossing, and rest my fingertip on her nipple. She gasps. Then I gasp. Fuck, it's beautiful. I hold it between my fingers while it grows stiff. I roll it to hear her moan. I want the other nipple, too. I pull the V until the other exquisite breast breaks free. Who survives this? Who doesn't start sucking and nibbling right away? I start sucking and nibbling and Thena has thrown her head back, her neck exposed, her lips parted. I wrap my legs around hers so she doesn't fall off the sofa. My mouth goes to her neck. Fingers from both hands pulling on these mysteries, piecing together the moans and the mumbled words. I think I hear my name. I think I feel her hands on my own skin, digging into my waist, pulling my pelvis against hers while my legs continue to keep her off the floor. I want to see the skin below her breasts, on the sides, I want to look at her navel, touch the skin on her stomach. Is she soft all over? I grab the bottom of her T-shirt, "Take this off, Thena." She sits up quickly, yanks the shirt off her body, tosses it behind her. Then hovers above me, a nipple teasing my lips. We are in a glowing dark. I need to make a change. I need her under me immediately, to press her into this sofa, get inside her. She begins to protest when I extract myself from our tangle to remove my clothes but goes still when she realizes what I'm doing.*

"Is this really happening?" she asks as she stares hard at my emerging body.

"This is absolutely happening," I say with something completely fierce and my own taking over. "I'm going to fuck you until we're both exhausted, even though I don't yet know how to do that. I mean . . . I know. I can guess, but I probably won't be as good as I'll be later." Okay, maybe not completely fierce.

Her smile burns and nourishes, "That sounds good. But be advised we're fucking each other to exhaustion. Like a team."

And we do. And we win.

I: You did not just conclude that totally sexy scene with a sports reference.

R: Well, the alternative is:

And there it was, that last piece of the puzzle—a puzzle she'd only recently realized she was constructing—clicking into place.

I: Wrong tense, wrong point of view.

R: But you know what I mean. You can't write a romance without referencing puzzle pieces at least once. That final piece that completes you, sealing a couple in their HEA.

I: So, you're done?

R: I don't think so. Not yet.

I: Since you bypassed all that fleeing and departing the country stuff, what's left?

R: It just depends on whether we think Thena and June need to go through some kind of trial before we believe they're set for life. I'm definitely not into the Happy for Now sentiment. I want my people walking off into the sunset.

I: Well, a puzzle doesn't fit together one day, then not fit the next.

R: That's true. That's very true. Let me see . . . I guess I want to think about what remains, like, in the field, after they have walked off, and maybe too a little bit about what the reader might need. Although readers are hard to account for, as is whichever book of yours they're reading. It never happens that the book they're reading is precisely the one you wrote. Add to that the chaos of writing a book within a book within a third book that's practically invisible.

I: Wait, there's a third book? Since when, and why is this the first time we're discussing it?

R: It's hard to know when to bring up the invisible book. Yet it seems a disservice to tell a story of writing and only talk about the books you can see. You've got to at least acknowledge the other books that are present. Especially in a book about writing. So, yes, there is a third book that holds the first two, that grants the fiction of the second. We obtain to fiction because of the unseen book that encompasses us. It's not completely invisible. You can feel it at the edges.

I: What do we know about this book?

R: Part of the reason it remains invisible is because it's nearly impossible to put into words the work it does. It's not there to be linguistic.

I: Then, how do you know it's there?

R: When you realize that an interview can be a novel, can be fictional, but also expository. And you realize this because of a moment where something curls over something else, a word folds over another, the edges of one of the visible books makes that rustling sound, like leaves in trees. When the romance rustles, we talk about it in the interview. When the interview rustles, I turn around in my chair and say something to Danielle. We walk the woods or leave for vacation without telling the book, either of the books, but I think about the book the whole time I'm away. I wonder about the end. I keep my research going, looking for sentiments in the world. The third book, the book on the outer layer, allows the second book—where we are—space to wonder and to be a "true account" fictionally. I'm sure there's an equation for this.

I: Before we got sidetracked by the invisible book, which maybe is just another way to talk about authorship, you were talking about what remains of the romance after June and Thena have walked off into the sunset. Shall we return to that?

R: Sure, but just to say: if we call the third book authorship, then it's authorship-in-a-room, which is basically what instigates fiction in the first place. So, it's a book. The third of three or the first, depending on how you're counting. But, I also think there's more to it than that. I haven't talked at all about my obsession with outer space. I don't know if you think about it, but it's on my mind all the time. The Delta Quadrant, for example. Just because it was featured in *Star Trek: Voyager* doesn't mean it doesn't exist. There is definitely a quadrant of space so far away that even at warp speed, which I'm very disappointed we don't have yet, it would take almost eighty years to reach, or, in the case of the Voyager, to get home from. In any case—I must have said this in another interview because I feel like I'm repeating myself, like almost verbatim—when I try to encompass that space, try to hold the shape of eighty years of space at warp seven or eight, it just breaks everything. In a beautiful and exciting way. That's how I think of the invisible book, which happens because of an opposite problem of the universe. It's because of a tiny fracture in the fabric of writing that the novel of writing exists. For me, that fracture is as enticingly imponderable as is trying to grasp the shape of the universe. I have always been in awe and deeply unsettled by the way the self flickers in the unfolding of sentences. I imagine the invisible book is where the flicker takes place. But, I know you get nervous when we get too close to the architecture—or is it better to say physics—of our own talking, so I'll leave the invisible book here.

As for what remains, it's questions mostly. I have never reached the end of a book like this before. What do I do with all these loose ends, like the Detroit House? Does it matter whether June finishes that project? Or is it just a symbol of the ongoing of her work life? What about the brown women drawing in various locations throughout the city? Are they hallucinations? Signs in the field to point to Thena? Suggestions for future expression within June's own practice? Are the women related to the mushrooms? Does everyone have a reading of the mushrooms that they're happy with? Do June and Thena need to have more sex? Should I talk about slickness and penetration and nubs and "rosebuds"? I encountered this word in a book today. Does the reader want me to narrate their orgasms? I did make a big deal about those descriptions earlier. Shouldn't Thena meet June's best friends? Esther will love her by the way. Did I say that already? And, lastly, should Thena get a tempting offer to do some kind of work that would require her to move back to London, setting her up to make a choice for her future? The tension would be short-lived though, because June would go with her, no questions. She's in her mushrooms, never letting go now that she understands them. And now she has someone she needs to protect, which seems grounding for her. I'm not really sure why we're so in favor of showing over telling. Isn't it refreshing just to hear how things are without having to endure them? And what about Thena's last name? June's? Do we need to know them?

I: At this point, I'm not sure what we would do with that information if we had it. I guess people who crave detail may be left wanting. But they've probably been wanting this whole time. What about the must-have scenes you mentioned earlier, that are foundational to a good romance? Want to narrate a few of those?

R: Yes! Here is one of my favorites: for some reason the potential couple is sleeping in the same house but in separate rooms; sometime in the middle of the night, one of the women is awakened by strange sounds coming from somewhere in the house. It sounds like a struggle. She gets up and tracks the sound to the room where the other MC is sleeping; the other is having a nightmare. The first woman, not having a nightmare, reacts immediately. Any of these scenarios gets my eyes filling up: she wakes her gently and consoles; she grabs her, holds her tight, and consoles; she picks her up, carries her to her own bed, and consoles.

I: Any others you want to share?

R: I'm not sure I want people to know how thoroughly mushy I can be. I wonder if I'll look back on this one and call it my menopause book.

I: You did say you were in your middle life.

R: I did.

I: You also promised me a list of your favorite romances. Can we get that before we close?

R: Can I give you one, one that I think I'll still love when this book comes out? It's called *Without Words* by Cameron Darrow. The author has written one of the best characters I've read across all genres. Her name is Zifa. Her origins are complex: she's born elven, abandoned for some reason by her parents who throw her into a magic pool, perhaps as a sacrifice, and a dragon saves her but in so doing alters Zifa's biology. When she's returned to her people, she is half white and half bronze, split right down the middle, with two different color eyes. And on the left side of her body she has talons instead of nails on her hands and feet and a horn on her head. Her people don't know what to make of her; they let her stay, but she grows up an outsider. Only one person cares for her, the warrior of the village. One thing I love about Zifa, or the way she's written, is her speech. Because of the dragon magic—I'm giving spoilers at this point—her thoughts form and disperse much faster than her ability to articulate them. She uses a stuttered, pared-down language that no one, except the warrior, has the patience to discern, and she only understands herself, expresses herself from the third person. These elves live in trees, travel by bridges from tree to tree, and rarely are on the ground. Zifa stands out further because rather than using the bridges, she swings and flies among trees like a monkey. She's very stealth, so often others don't know when she's around. She eavesdrops on conversations, hanging upside down from branches, trying to figure out what's going on since hardly anyone takes the time to communicate with her. It's easy as a reader to find Zifa endearing and root for her. But the story really takes off when an Amazonian elven princess from the desert lands shows up with her entourage to ask the forest elves to help them with an environmental crisis. The queen of the forest elves is a brat and won't help them, so things get tense. The princess—her name is Skathi—notices Zifa immediately, sees her worth, treats her with respect, which blows Zifa's mind, further endearing her to the reader, and the two of them set out on an adventure through a volcanic mountain and a swath of dangerously uninhabitable desert to save Skathi's people. The desert elves find Zifa fascinating and embrace her immediately. Many things happen, some secrets are revealed, the desert elves are saved, and in the midst of that Skathi falls for Zifa, and Zifa undergoes a further transformation that makes her look even stranger. That's probably my favorite part. She doesn't get "fixed," she gets empowered.

I: That sounds like a novel I'd want to read. I love elves and dragons and don't run across them too often in literary fiction. Also, I'm not surprised that you'd love a book like this, as you've been saying all along that you look for narratives where people get the care they need. What about something among your favorites that isn't fantasy or adventure based?

R: Hmm. There's a novella I adore that I've read a few times that's more of a light read. It uses the well-worn "woke up in Vegas drunk-married" motif but has a sweet twist that pulls my obviously very responsive heart strings. The book is called *Help! I Married a Straight Girl!* by Annabeth Leong. Two women wake up in a hotel room, naked, smelling of sex, severely hungover, and, as they soon discover, married. Pam is a lesbian, vacationing alone in Vegas after a recent breakup; Kris is straight, traveling with a boyfriend. She wants to marry him, but he's reluctant, and she's hoping this trip will make a difference to him. They had a fight the previous night; then she met Pam and shit hit the fan. At least, that's how it feels when they wake up, because they can't remember events from the previous night, and Kris maintains she's straight. What's clear from the few scraps of memory they have, especially from Pam's perspective, is that they had a lot of hot sex— the room is a mess, they taste each other in their mouths, etc. Pam is interested in getting to know Kris, but Kris is freaking out and needs to get back to her hotel and confess to her boyfriend what's happened. That's the part of the story that's expected. The boyfriend is an asshole, and nobody feels sorry for him, even though Kris did cheat on him, and as I said earlier I don't love that. But what gets to me about the way the story unfolds is that Pam and Kris never take off their rings. They're trying to figure out what happened and to undo it, but at the same time both have this kind of trust in themselves that there must have been a reason that they married each other, even if they were stupid drunk. The story takes place over just a couple of days, so it's kind of an insta-love romance, but by the end of the second day they've tracked down a copy of the actual wedding ceremony and the clarity of their intent and readiness is so obvious they stop questioning why they've done this outrageous thing. Somehow, they know. It's terribly sentimental, isn't it? How will I live down exposing this utter need I have for lesbian love stories? But, look, it's so big it's totally spilled over into my literary life. Made a mess of my autobiography.

I: I'm so glad I've been here to witness it. I'm intrigued, though. You love these books even though you find them poorly written?

R: Well, the two I've just described are actually very competently written, but yes there are a bunch I've re-read many times that are full of dull and terrible sentences. Remarkably, just a few weeks ago, I was talking with a friend, who is the only literary writer I know that also has a successful career as a romance writer, under a pen name, of course, so there are probably more of them out there. Anyway, she and I were having a moment about how we both are drawn to romance despite the quality of a lot of the writing; we wondered if this had to do with the characters themselves, as if they embody alluring qualities or needs or questions that exist independent of how they're written. Reading, then, would be like looking through a dirty window: the characters are legible in a way that defies the obstructed view. Sometimes, while I'm reading, I apologize to the character. I say, "I'm sorry, honey, I think I know what you mean. I see what you're trying to do." Or I stare and stare through the grime and kind of rewrite where they are or what they're saying. Not in words exactly. I'm not rewriting these stories in my own language. Rather, it's more like I want to hum some air or drift into the space, something flowing. Maybe this happens when people watch bad TV, too; they sort of soften the eyes, tilt the laptop, manipulate the speed of the playback. I keep thinking I'm going to reach the end of wanting to read these stories. That I'll fill up on these repeating storylines of people finding the one person or the found family that nourishes them, but here I am still eating.

I: Here you are. We'll close the book and you'll still be flickering.

R: That's true.

I: Anything else to add before we close this?

R: Well, you never did say how your date went? And what about your 600-page novel? How will you finish it?

ACKNOWLEDGMENTS

Because I'm a compulsive confessor, I must say that sometimes, in the writing of this book, I experienced the interviewer as an amalgam of the sweet, attentive, and intelligent men who've passed through my life, a few having actually interviewed me for one journal or another, but the rest just good friends and collaborators. I hope you know who you are because, though I love you, I cannot possibly fill up the last page of my lesbian novel with your names.

A curated excerpt from *My Lesbian Novel* was published in *The Paris Review*'s summer issue (2024). Many thanks to Emily Stokes and Oriana Ullman for their insights and enthusiasm.

While otherwise not previously published, in February 2019 *The Believer* (Issue 123) published a conversation between the writer and translator Anna Moschovakis and me, where I discussed the writing of *My Lesbian Novel* (all twenty-six pages of it at the time) in detail. In fact, for many years, I believed that would be the only public life *MLN* would have. Many thanks to *The Believer* and most especially to my friend, Anna, whom I also sometimes see in I, the interviewer.

Also thank you to Joanna Ruocco for that beautifully expansive conversation we had about romances.

And thanks and love to the interlocutors and ted-talkers in my life: EJ Colon, Joanna Howard, John Cayley, Jessica Lanyadoo, Mary Ruefle, Kate Briggs, my sisters Vanessa and Gwen, and Amy Peterson.

And always to Danielle Dutton and Martin Riker of Dorothy.

And always always to Danielle Vogel.

RENEE GLADMAN is an artist preoccupied with crossings, thresholds, and geographies as they play out at the intersections of writing, drawing, and architecture. She is the author of numerous published works, including a cycle of novels about the city-state Ravicka and its inhabitants, the Ravickians—*Event Factory* (2010), *The Ravickians* (2011), *Ana Patova Crosses a Bridge* (2013), and *Houses of Ravicka* (2017)—all published by Dorothy. Recent essays and visual work have appeared in *The Architectural Review*, *POETRY*, *The Paris Review*, *The Yale Review*, and *e-flux*, in addition to several artist monographs and exhibition catalogs. Gladman's first solo exhibition of drawings, *The Dreams of Sentences*, opened in fall 2022 at Wesleyan University, followed by *Narratives of Magnitude* at Artists Space in New York City in spring 2023. She has been awarded fellowships and artist residencies from the Menil Drawing Institute, Harvard Radcliffe Institute, Foundation for Contemporary Arts, among others, and received a Windham-Campbell prize in fiction in 2021. She makes her home in New England.

1. Renee Gladman *Event Factory*
2. Barbara Comyns *Who Was Changed and Who Was Dead*
3. Renee Gladman *The Ravickians*
4. Manuela Draeger *In the Time of the Blue Ball* (tr. Brian Evenson)
5. Azareen Van der Vliet Oloomi *Fra Keeler*
6. Suzanne Scanlon *Promising Young Women*
7. Renee Gladman *Ana Patova Crosses a Bridge*
8. Amina Cain *Creature*
9. Joanna Ruocco *Dan*
10. Nell Zink *The Wallcreeper*
11. Marianne Fritz *The Weight of Things* (tr. Adrian Nathan West)
12. Joanna Walsh *Vertigo*
13. Nathalie Léger *Suite for Barbara Loden* (tr. Natasha Lehrer & Cécile Menon)
14. Jen George *The Babysitter at Rest*
15. Leonora Carrington *The Complete Stories*
16. Renee Gladman *Houses of Ravicka*
17. Cristina Rivera Garza *The Taiga Syndrome* (tr. Aviva Kana & Suzanne Jill Levine)
18. Sabrina Orah Mark *Wild Milk*
19. Rosmarie Waldrop *The Hanky of Pippin's Daughter*
20. Marguerite Duras *Me & Other Writing* (tr. Olivia Baes & Emma Ramadan)
21. Nathalie Léger *Exposition* (tr. Amanda DeMarco)
22. Nathalie Léger *The White Dress* (tr. Natasha Lehrer)
23. Cristina Rivera Garza *New and Selected Stories* (tr. Sarah Booker, et al)
24. Caren Beilin *Revenge of the Scapegoat*
25. Amina Cain *A Horse at Night: On Writing*
26. Giada Scodellaro *Some of Them Will Carry Me*
27. Pip Adam *The New Animals*
28. Kate Briggs *The Long Form*
29. Ariane Koch *Overstaying* (tr. Damion Searls)
30. Renee Gladman *My Lesbian Novel*
31. Renee Gladman *To After That (TOAF)*